'The sea is glorio s
watched it for days just
touched it.'

Nick drifted closer until he could brush her
hand. 'Mmm. I feel the same.'

She opened her eyes lazily and paddled with
her hands until she bumped into his chest.
'Oops. Sorry.'

'Don't be.' His hands captured her shoulders
and pulled her slowly into his chest, so that she
was anchored on his lap in the water. 'I'm a sea
god. You have to pay a tax when you bump into
me.'

She closed one eye. 'Well, I'm a mermaid. Do
you have any idea how dangerous I am?'

Oh, yes. She was dangerous, all right—much
more than a woman who knew the rules—but
still he turned her to face him.

'I laugh at danger,' he said, and she giggled
again.

So he kissed her, which was what he'd wanted
to do since she'd met him on the gangplank this
morning, and time stood still and her skin felt
like silk under the water as she twined her arms
around his neck.

When she returned his kiss with such an
innocent ardour it tore at his heart and tightened
his chest. He couldn't remember when it had
been like this.

*Holding Tara was precious, yet terrifying,
and some of that fear was a residual warning
against becoming too fond of someone.*

**Dear Reader**

Have you ever been on a sea voyage? Or imagined being on one? Had moments when you lean on the rail and gaze out over an ocean that stretches away to the horizon?

I've always wanted to write a cruise ship love story, and have been fascinated by the staff who work in those mini-hospitals below decks. There was even a handsome single doc on my cruise, who showed us around, and I've been itching to write his story.

So meet my two shipboard doctors: Nick and Tara.

Tara has been working as an aid doctor under primitive conditions in the Sudan and is being forced to have a break. She just doesn't expect to end up as a doctor on a cruise liner.

Nick Fender loves to party. He was the only man in the house with four fabulous sisters, and he has no wish to settle down. Nick's on holiday at the moment, but working as a cocktail waiter on the *Sea Goddessa*, filling in for his youngest sis Kiki, who has pneumonia. It's a job he once did himself when he took a break from medicine. (Watch out for Kiki's story coming soon!)

Our voyage sails Nick and Tara around the magnificent Mediterranean, and they discover each other's strengths as they pass the Greek Isles, the coast of Italy, Croatia and finally Venice. Venice… Ahh… I hope you have fun as we sail away on the fantasy of the *Sea Goddessa* and the emotional journey of Nick and Tara.

With warmest wishes

*Fiona*

# A DOCTOR,
# A FLING &
# A WEDDING RING

BY
FIONA McARTHUR

First published in Great Britain 2012
by Mills & Boon, an imprint of Harlequin (UK) Limited.
Large Print edition 2013
Harlequin (UK) Limited, Eton House,
18-24 Paradise Road, Richmond, Surrey TW9 1SR

© Fiona McArthur 2012

ISBN: 978 0 263 23104 5

Printed and bound in Great Britain
by CPI Antony Rowe, Chippenham, Wiltshire

Mother to five sons, **Fiona McArthur** is an Australian midwife who loves to write. Medical Romance™ gives Fiona the scope to write about all the wonderful aspects of adventure, romance, medicine and midwifery that she feels so passionate about—as well as an excuse to travel! Now that her boys are older, Fiona and her husband, Ian, are off to meet new people, see new places, and have wonderful adventures. Fiona's website is at www.fionamcarthur.com

**Also by Fiona McArthur:**

**Praise for
Fiona McArthur:**

'McArthur does full justice to an intensely emotional scene of the delivery of a stillborn baby—one that marks a turning point in both the characters' outlooks. The entire story is liberally spiced with drama, heartfelt emotion and just a touch of humour.'
—*RT Book Reviews* on
SURVIVAL GUIDE TO DATING YOUR BOSS

**These books are also available in eBook format
from www.millsandboon.co.uk**

To Rosie, my shipmate,
who made it possible.

# CHAPTER ONE

TARA MCWILLIAMS walked away from the tent but the whispering sobs of grief from the widower followed her like the relentless harshness of Africa followed her clients. The sound of heartbreak. Losing a young wife and child because by the time they'd walked here it had been too late for Tara to be able to help.

A tiny insect flew into her eye and as she brushed it away she wished she could summon up some tears. Doug's hand rested gently on her shoulder and she reached up to cover the wrinkled skin, offering comfort. Just to feel life beneath her fingers.

Douglas Curlew squeezed her shoulder. 'You're done, Tara. No more.'

Tara pushed the limp hair off her forehead and sighed as Doug's fingers fell away. 'I'm fine.'

Doug glanced back over his shoulder towards the tent. 'You're not fine, you're mentally exhausted, physically frail and need to get away from here for at least six months, if not permanently. Two years battling to save lives here is enough. Vander wouldn't have expected it.'

'We both know he would have.' She glanced around at the grimy greyness of the tent city. The harsh sun beat down on them from overhead and she shielded her eyes. 'And I'm not the one who's left crying.'

'Maybe you should be. When was the last time you let yourself go?'

A trickle of sweat rolled between her breasts and skittered down to her belly. Not much cleavage there to stop it any more. She lifted her head wearily. 'I haven't cried since he died. No time for useless emotion here, is there?' Tara thought about that and sighed again.

For the first time she glimpsed the truth in Doug's words. Her body ached with the lethargy of deep exhaustion. She had no doubt she could sleep where she fell.

She almost couldn't remember why she stayed here. 'You know as well as I do, Doug, we're critically understaffed. Who would do my job if I didn't? That's why Vander wanted me to stay.'

Doug shrugged philosophically. 'Vander died eighteen months ago.' He was more grounded to reality than Tara. 'Who did the job before you both came?' He shrugged. 'The same person who'll do your job if you burn out completely. The fact is, you're different from the vibrant young woman you used to be.'

Her chief patted her shoulder and gestured to the sea of tents in the refugee evacuation camp. 'You've done an incredible job for too long.

This place has grown from five thousand to eighty thousand. The emergency birth procedures you've taught are saving countless lives that would have been lost. The staff you trained will carry on, but they love you and they're worried, and they're entitled to care enough to ask you to rest.'

It was almost too much effort to lift her shoulders in a shrug. 'Okay. I'll rest.'

Doug's dog-with-a-bone worrying became even more tenacious. 'Have a decent holiday at least. A total change of scene.'

'And do what?' Tara threw out her hands. 'I've seen so many tragedies here I don't think I could stop and just sit. Images of all those brave women who've died would revolve in my head like a horror film.'

'That's exactly what I mean.' He lowered his thick white Scottish brows and his brogue softened and shifted like the sand beneath their feet.

'Time to go, Tara. Find a little light relief. I've seen staff crash and burn and you're close. I don't want that for you.'

And do what? she thought again. Her parents were gone. No significant other. That was a laugh. 'I can't just sit. Do nothing. My house is rented, I don't have a job, there's nothing in Australia for me.' Sure, she was different from the wanting-to-do-good and eager-to-learn young woman of two years ago. You couldn't stay enthusiastic and fresh when you saw birthing women stoically accept they would die because they lived in the wrong part of the world.

'You don't have to go all the way home.' He rubbed his chin. 'Been thinking about that. I've a friend who captains a cruise liner due to sail in three days from Rome. Twelve days at a time and their junior doctor broke his leg. He's willing to rush the paperwork.'

For the first time in a long time Tara felt like

laughing but the tinge of hysteria she could feel in her throat gave her pause. Shakily she gathered her control, like grasping at the string of a kite that almost got away. 'You're not talking change, Doug, you're talking a different planet.'

Tara grimaced and tried to imagine herself caring for pampered cruise-line passengers after the horrors she'd seen here in the Sudan. 'You know how many women out of every thousand women die having babies here, Doug. How could I move to a luxury liner?'

'It's the quickest option I can think of. The cruise is less than two weeks long. Then they'll drop you off in Venice, where they can replace the crew doctor and you can fly home or wherever you want. Or you could stay on and have a working holiday.'

Venice? She'd always wanted to see Venice.

She shook her head. Incomprehensible.

'And you wouldn't be treating the passengers

as your main priority—the unfortunate guy was the junior and you'd be caring for the crew. The senior would do most of the passenger liaison.'

Still. A luxury liner? After this? 'I don't think so.'

Doug stared her down. Not something he would've been able to do a year ago. 'It's not a suggestion, Tara.'

'Are you ordering me to leave?' She raised her brows but her voice wasn't as steady as she would have liked.

'Yes. And if I could, I'd order you to indulge in a random dalliance with a cocktail waiter or gym instructor and really let your hair down.' Doug had one hand on his hips and the other in the air, admonishing.

Now she did laugh and it sounded almost natural. 'And I always thought of you as a father figure. I can't ever imagine my father telling me to get laid.'

His finger dropped. 'I didn't say that.' He smiled as he continued, 'But maybe treating yourself to a bit of pampering, indulging yourself for a week or two, go all out on the massage and happy hour when you're off duty. I would love to picture that when you drive away.'

'I'll think about it.' Nice dream. Last thing she could imagine but she could pretend.

But Tara's world shifted as Doug laid down the law. 'Your driver will be here in the Jeep in four hours to take you to the airport. You fly to Rome, sleep for an extra day, and pick up the ship there. You should have enough time to pack and say goodbye.'

Tara felt the cold wash of reality, of change, and a little of the trepidation new places caused in a woman who just might have forgotten how to be a woman. And just a tiny whisper of relief. She really was getting close to the edge. 'I can't leave just like that.'

He looked at her kindly. 'Can I tell you, in my experience, when you've invested as much as you have into this place and with these people, it's the only way to leave?'

# CHAPTER TWO

TWO DAYS later at eleven a.m. Tara stood on the dock in Civitavecchia, Rome's nearby port for cruise ships. Apart from the blinding white cruise liner that dominated the dock, it wasn't a romantic place, more a service centre with cranes and cargo ships and a semi-deserted building more reminiscent of a warehouse than a cruise-liner departure hall. Well, that was good. She wasn't feeling in the least romantic.

The officer in white asked her business and she handed over the papers Doug had given her.

'Welcome to the *Sea Goddess*, Dr McWilliams. I'll page Dr Hobson to meet you as soon as you board. If you would move through to check in via Security, please.'

'Thank you.' What the heck was she doing here?

* * *

Nick Fender, temporary bar manager for the Sea Goddess, decided the hardship of holding his sister's job for her wasn't so bad.

The sounds and subtle shift of the moored cruise ship soaked into his smile. It had been a while since he'd done a stint on a ship, as ship's doctor last time. It had been even longer since the early days when he'd had a year off from med school after his parents had died and worked as the cocktail waiter everyone had loved. That's when he'd laid the foundations for the life-of-the-party persona he'd grown very comfortable with.

So here he was back behind the bar, selling cocktails and holding down Kiki's job while she fought off pneumonia. Wilhelm, the current ship's doctor, had thought Nick's retro-vocation hilarious and Nick was starting to see the funny side of it too.

And then there were the women. Some men could develop an ease with the opposite sex and

Nick was one of them. He loved women. No favouritism.

That was until he glimpsed the tall, fine-boned dolly bird arrive late to the briefing room, and judging by her uniform she was the ship's new junior doctor.

An uneasy prickle of déjà vu kept his eyes on her but he'd remember if he'd seen her before. But something was there. Something about her that tweaked at all the protective instincts he hadn't known he had, at some gut level of awareness.

Nick loved the female gender. His doting sisters probably had something to do with that, and Nick liked to dip and dally, like the seagulls he could see outside the porthole, because he wasn't falling for the have-and-hold dream. His parents' early deaths and the letter he could tell no one about had seen to that.

Nick laughed his way through life with like-minded friends, and there were a lot of those working cruise liners. It was all about avoiding the horror of being left with just one person for ever.

Until she walked in. What the hell was that? He dragged his eyes away and concentrated on his watch to work out when the first passengers would arrive, when the ship would sail out the harbour, and when the bar would open. He didn't have time for some random woman to explode unexpectedly like fine champagne on his frothy beer life.

He was the good-time guy.

Tara glanced around the small room filled with chairs and smiling crew members and started towards a seat in front of the hunky guy in the back row. He had those laughing black eyes all the best pirate actors had, the ones who could crook their little fingers at buxom wenches who'd come running.

Well, nobody would call her buxom. She'd lost so much weight she'd left her breasts in the Sudan and now for the first time she almost missed them.

He looked away as she caught his eye and she thought of her boss, Doug, and for the first time today a small smile tugged at her mouth. The smile broadened as she got closer, read his badge and realised he was actually a bar manager. Doug had said find a cocktail waiter so she was going up in the world.

Not that she really wanted to have an affair. Being the merry widow wasn't her style but she did need to relearn how to talk to people. How to talk to men. That was, men who weren't relatives of women who'd died or Doug.

She'd grown up enough not to expect to find 'romantic love'. Vander had laughed at that. Still, maybe she could practise her smiles and small talk and become a normal socially acceptable human being again.

She'd at least managed to have her cracked and broken nails attended to and her hair cut this morning at the hotel. She really would try to lighten up for a week or two as ordered because even with the twenty-four hours' sleep she'd had she was starting to feel better.

Maybe Doug had been right and she did need to touch the other world out there.

Her immediate superior on ship, Wilhelm Hobson, had met her at the gangplank and given her a quick orientation tour. Big ship! No doubt she'd be hopelessly lost for a few more days and planned on sticking to the crew areas and the medical centre to keep her bearings.

She certainly didn't want to flirt with Wilhelm. The last thing Tara needed was to discuss work socially, apart from the fact doctors and death went together in her mind at the moment. She didn't want to flirt with anyone but she would like to meet people she could talk with and, heaven forbid, even laugh with after the uneven fight she'd been waging for the last two years.

She sighed and wrenched her mind away from the camp. Concentrate on the here and now, she reminded herself.

The ship's medical centre, much larger than she'd expected, seemed almost obscenely stocked with equipment after her workplace at the camp. Apart from three consulting rooms and ten observation inpatient beds, the centre even had its own X-ray machine. And morgue. She frowned at herself.

There were ECGs, defibrillators, minor surgical equipment and orthopaedic immobilisation gear. No doubt all would be useful, along with the myriad general-practice skills that would be needed in this isolated community far from land.

It actually did promise to be interesting the more she blocked her mind from her desertion of the refugee camp. In fact, perhaps not a bad way to ease back into the general-practice headspace she'd need to revisit for the next six months. That was how long Doug had stipulated before he would even consider her return.

The dashing young South African physician in charge was sweet, and obviously a bit of a player, but if she wanted to learn people skills, she wanted light, frivolously very far from medicine, and definitely short term. Just so she could show Doug she was fine.

So here she was and she resisted the evil urge to sneak another peek at the heady masculine brew behind her. Way out of her league but maybe she could make up a drink name for him. Unfortunately the ones that popped into her head tinged on the Curacao blue side and she mentally backed away.

What had got into her?

She hadn't expected to leap onto Doug's idea with a vengeance. Bizarre when she hadn't looked at a man since med school and look where that had left her. A widow in a refugee camp with shoulders full of guilt for being the one who'd survived.

She'd never even been a necessary part of her parents' lives, and Vander had said he needed her. Actually, as a missionary he'd needed her skills, so she'd flown off with her new husband filled with the warm and fuzzy idea that he'd loved her. Reality had left her bewildered but before she'd been able to get too angry at him for not being interested in love and sex, apparently the last thing he needed after a fifteen-hour day, he'd died of cholera.

So two years down the track was that what she wanted? Sex? Would that fix her? Make her human again?

Because she certainly felt robotic with years of bounding out of bed after ten minutes' sleep, crash Caesareans with one eye open, triplets before breakfast, and massive post-partum haemorrhages at least once a night.

She'd have to stay awake for it, of course. Sex. She'd never really had the chance to figure what all the fuss was about. But one glance behind at corded muscles and mile-wide shoulders and she was contemplating caffeine to help keep her eyes open.

Good grief. She was seriously unstable and maybe Doug had it right. She chewed her lip to stop the smile. She felt decidedly immoral just thinking about it, and as a blush stole up her neck she glanced at her watch, willing the safety lecture to get going.

Safety seemed like a good thing to dwell on. That, and removing her mind from the gutter.

A shift in air currents and a sudden blocking of light was probably what had caused her breath to catch. That or the fact the intoxicating man behind had shifted and sat down beside her. Suddenly the room was two degrees hotter and filled with a crackling tension. So there really were men out there where that pheromone antenna thing actually happened and you got goose-bumps?

'Hello, there. You're new here?' Deep, skin-tingling voice that raised the hairs on the back of her neck and a whiff of some expensive cologne the price of which would probably feed a Sudanese family for a month. *Pleeease*. Tara fought the blush from her cheeks.

Nick had specifically told his legs no when they'd wanted to shift him forward one row and sit beside the too-thin brunette, but the force of nature was not to be reckoned with and by the time he'd settled in next to her he'd already accepted it. Just a conversation.

She raised thick brown eyebrows that disdained fashion. In fact, he smiled to himself as he thought of the women he knew and their fetish for perfect dyed and primped arches, he doubted these had ever seen a pair of tweezers. 'Do I look that new?'

He waggled his forehead. 'New. Lost. And very new….'

She glanced away. 'Thanks.'

'You're welcome.' She looked at him again and he grinned to show he was only kidding, but she didn't smile back. Crashed and burned, old boy, he mocked himself. 'And on that auspicious beginning perhaps we could introduce ourselves.'

He held out his hand and he'd have to say gingerly she put her fingers briefly in his. Maybe he should have assured her his were clean, judging by her reluctance.

'I'm Tara McWilliams.'

'Tara.' *The star-ar.* He always rhymed names

to remember. First rule of attracting women. Remember their names. Nick had never noticed hands during a handshake before. Not what you did, really, but hers…fingers, bone-slender, too cold. She looked a little anaemic, her hand so workworn that he had the bizarre impulse to rub it warm and shelter it between his palms.

Instead, he continued the conversation as if he hadn't noticed her pull herself free quickly. 'Nick. Bar manager for the Casablanca Bar.'

'Appropriate.'

He scratched his head comically and shook it. 'Don't get it?'

'Humphrey Bogart. Casablanca. His name was Nick in the movie.'

He grinned. 'Actually, it was Rick. Sorry. I have four sisters who love romantic movies but will henceforth think of Bogart every time I see my name now.'

She narrowed her eyes at him but not enough

to distract him from noticing the colour. Honey brown. Or toffee. Like her skin. Like her gorgeous legs and arms. Edible. And yet incredibly weary.

She folded her arms across her chest. 'Do you always correct people?' She was cross. And still looked good with it. Damn good.

He blinked and opened his eyes wide. 'Only when they're wrong.'

Tara had to laugh. Or be hurt because she wasn't used to people correcting her. It had all been life and death for the last two years with very little light relief and this barman had probably seen just the opposite. In fact, maybe she should cultivate him and relearn her humour and fluff from the fantasy world of shipboard existence. Good candidate.

'Don't worry. You'll have fun.' Could he read her mind?

She tasted the word. Rolled it around in her

mouth and nibbled at it. Fun. Imagine. She grimaced. Boy, was she out of practice.

This guy looked like he rolled in good times. Most likely shimmied in sex. 'I'll try.' She had no doubt he could provide her with more fun than even Doug would want for her if she made any effort at all. Scary thought but she'd been a reasonably fun person before she'd grown up.

The emergency drill session at the front of the room started and she sat up straight.

Nick watched her concentrate as the senior safety officer began to speak. So a serious pupil, determined to pay attention and learn all she could before the new influx of passengers arrived that afternoon. That was good.

He was interested too, had had a private introduction as a manager that had been more in-depth and he'd come along to see if his staff were attending, but there was no doubt he'd become distracted by the intensity that Tara gave to her own process of learning.

He sat forward and concentrated. Had to admit he was keen to see where she'd be deployed compared to him. He might just have to keep an eye on her.

He guessed he had the advantage, having worked on ships before. After he'd qualified he'd done a year as junior doctor on board the sister ship to this one, and had actually been instrumental in Wilhelm deciding to try the life. So his old friend owed him and he'd called in that favour to put a word in for his sister when she'd gone down with pneumonia.

But all they'd been able to manage was Nick replacing Kiki for the two weeks or her bar manager's job would go. Luckily for Kiki, he didn't mind. He'd been due for a holiday anyway.

His ex-girlfriend, Jasmin, had been getting way too serious and not been pleased to jet off from Rome to New York on her own. Hence the relief in his newly single status. Family came first and he made no apologies. Especially when it suited him.

His attention flicked back to the lecture. The safety officer discussed the routine of a compulsory muster for all passengers before they sailed and outlined the crew's duties as emergency officers. Not much had changed and he was glad to see he was on the same station as Tara.

With over three thousand passengers and one thousand crew members the ship would give enough opportunities for her to slip out of sight. He couldn't remember when he'd last been so aware of planning to 'bump into' a woman.

Usually it just happened—or not. Funny how he didn't feel the same relaxed acceptance of fate with this slip of a medic beside him. Must be because she looked so frail—in an I-can-look-after-myself way that dared him to mention it.

He wasn't saying a thing but he'd be watching for her.

But as the middle child and only male in the family, it was his job to make everyone smile. After his parents had died it had been even more reason to be the entertainer. He was still the entertainer. He could show this Tara a very good time.

Tara walked away from Nick Fender. Fender? She could imagine the guy with an air guitar, thrusting his hips and pretending.

She blinked. What? Had she left her brain back in that room? She concentrated on the directions to the hospital pinned to the wall in front of her.

She had to keep reminding herself she was at work. It was so strange without the need to rush from one emergency to the next.

With the help of the occasional map, Tara navigated two stairwells and a corridor and found her way back to the hospital where Marie, the head nurse, was shifting boxes of supplies.

'Let me help with that.' Tara hurried forward and helped lift the other side of an awkwardly shaped parcel Marie wanted on the desk.

The nurse brushed the hair out of her eyes when the parcel was safely stowed. 'Thanks, Tara. It's the new ECG machine. It wasn't heavy but, boy, was it awkward.'

'So what else can I do for you?' Tara glanced around. Boxes everywhere.

Marie grinned at her. 'Seriously, I'm just unpacking. First day is all about unpacking and stowing.'

Tara rubbed her hands. Activity would be excellent. 'Then I'll help. It's the best way to find where things live anyway. Can't be asking you where everything is all the time.'

The two women smiled at each other and Tara felt like she'd gone the first step to making at least one friend. 'Always happy to have help. Though you'll have to go through the crew's notes before we leave this afternoon. Those with illnesses they've notified us of, anyway.'

She gestured Tara through to the ward area and a sterile supply room. 'Reckon this will be the place that confuses you most.'

The storeroom was wall-to-wall shelves. She glanced around and Tara wondered if she'd get back to being as easy to talk to as Marie was. Her own conversation skills needed repolishing—just those few exchanges with air-guitar Nick had shown her that—and she wanted to fit in. Drop her doom-and-gloom mantle that had grown since she'd married and try at least to pretend to join in with 'normal' people.

The day passed swiftly, especially when the passengers came on board. Most of them looked as lost as Tara had been when she'd been out of the hospital but the mood was high and excited and totally different from the world Tara had just left.

Tara stood with Marie on the deck and watched the lines being cast off, then they eased away from the dock and maybe she could adjust to the sway of the ship and the routines on board. It was all so different from the hectic rush from one dire patient to the next.

Normally the clinic for passengers opened three times a day for two hours. The crew phoned down for quick access most of the time.

Today the passenger clinic would open once except for emergencies—most of which Wilhelm would deal with. Lovely change. She only dealt with occupational mishaps of the crew, minor illnesses among them, and passenger cabin calls when Wilhelm couldn't attend.

Even her cabin on the crew deck seemed outrageously luxurious compared to her tent at the camp. Air-conditioning and hot and cold running water and a porthole that was much larger than she'd expected and afforded an amazing view across the water. She just might be in heaven.

# CHAPTER THREE

WHEN Tara woke on her first morning they weren't even at sea. They'd docked at six a.m. She'd never got around to really studying the itinerary before she'd boarded, had been so busy finding routes and equipment that when she opened the blinds, pleasure craft and even a castle on a mountain seemed surreal. Here she was, peering out of her window at the glorious bay of Monte Carlo.

Another good night's sleep had lightened her step and she found herself smiling as passengers oohed and ahhed over the rich and famous playground off which they'd anchored. There was something amazingly special about sitting at anchor on a floating hotel adjacent to a charming principality.

When Tara walked into the clinic waiting room she found it surprisingly busy for a day in port until she realised that most passengers wanted their tests and injections before they left on the tenders heading for shore.

When she offered to help with the backlog, Marie sent her in a young mother and her small son.

The woman was petite, perfectly coiffed and immaculately dressed. 'I'm Gwen, and this is my son, Tommy.' The woman patted his head and touched her son's forehead. 'I'm so worried. He's got spots. He's not contagious, is he?'

I sincerely hope not, Tara thought as she looked down at the little boy. 'Hello, Tommy.' Tara bent down and the little boy held out his hand for Tara to shake. His skin wasn't hot or dry and his eyes were clear.

'Is he getting German measles? He has spots,' his mother said again, clasping and unclasping her hands, and Tara felt the pull of sympathy for Tommy and his obviously distressed mum.

'You poor thing. Imagine that on the first day of your holiday. But I think he's fine. It may be a heat rash. Does he seem unwell to you?' She looked at the reading from the digital thermometer she'd just used in Tommy's ear.

Tara had seen more than enough German measles to be fairly certain this wasn't a case. The rash wasn't typical, barely visible and mildly pink, and the little boy didn't present as being unwell, but she gave the mother a list of other signs and suggested she bring him back if they manifested.

The mother nodded her head with concern. 'He's normally a little terror. Are you sure the spots are okay?'

'Yes, but you did the right thing bringing him

in to check. Especially if he's going into the child activity centre.'

Gwen shook her head vehemently. 'Oh, no. I'd never do that. There's just the two of us. His dad left us, you see, and we're visiting my sister in Mykonos on holiday. Sometimes he's not a well little boy and on the ship I don't have to travel without being safe. It's Tommy's holiday too.'

Tara smiled at the pair. 'He's very lucky to have you. Bring him back if you're worried, Gwen.'

Tara showed them out and Marie sent in an older lady who wanted her ear looked at for wax. Marie was chewing her lip, trying not to laugh, and Tara pretended to frown at her. This was not life-threatening stuff at all but the waiting room was emptying. Still no crew and at this rate they'd be clear of patients before the two hours was up.

Wilhelm was still sequestered with his previous patient so Tara took the older lady in with her.

Wilhelm and Tara had planned to catch up on the in-service needed with the new ECG machine, as well as go through the cases from the day before, and Marie planned to venture ashore to peep into the casino in Monaco.

Tara couldn't help but wonder what a certain bar-staff member was doing because most of the bars were shut when the cruise ship was in port. No doubt by the end of the cruise she'd have a fair idea. She even toyed with the idea of looking for him after tea, she'd seen the bar on the wall directions, but a swell came up and the hospital was inundated with motion-sickness sufferers and that put paid to that. Good thing too.

On the second morning when Tara woke they were tied to the wharf at Livorno, the gateway to Florence, the leaning tower of Pisa and Tuscany, none of which she'd seen. Or would.

But Tara was off duty later in the morning and quite happy to explore the less-crowded ship.

She ventured through the main passenger areas in civilian clothes and gazed around at the surprising throng of passengers foregoing the shore excursions.

Up in the sunlight, at one of the few open bars on board, Nick lorded it behind the Casablanca Bar like a sheikh in a harem. Tara stepped back behind one of the ship's columns on the swimming-pool deck and watched him work.

She had to admit he filled his blue T-shirt admirably and the muscles in his chest and those arms were blatantly provocative as he shook his cocktail shaker and grinned at the world.

Why weren't these women off visiting the city where they were docked? The rattle of ice carried across the hum of conversations that floated above the deckchairs and his teeth flashed as he theatrically poured the contents into a glass from a great height without a splash.

Well, she guessed Nick was one reason. She had to cover her mouth to stop herself laughing out loud, which kind of surprised her because the little bubble of excitement that surfaced just by seeing him was totally unexpected.

She frowned and looked away but there was nothing quite as much fun to look at. She couldn't dispute she was feeling better than she had been when she'd stepped on board but this guy was nobody to her. And she was certainly a nobody to him.

Her gaze drifted back to Nick as he scooped up a decorative skewer of pineapple and cherry and garnished a creation with a flamboyant wave.

He was so confident, Tara could feel her lips tug again, so clearly a showman and ladies' man, she probably didn't have a hope of practising her extremely rusty wiles on him, but if she got the chance, at least it meant he couldn't be hurt if she did get to first base with him.

Still she hung back. Watched the woman he'd served walk away with an exaggerated wiggle, and noted with approval Nick's attention was on cleaning his cocktail equipment, not on her bikini bottom. So he took the rules for consorting with passengers seriously. She'd been surprised how severely intimacy with passengers was dealt with on the ship. No doubt instant dismissal wouldn't look good on his résumé.

Or maybe he just wasn't interested. He didn't look gay. At all. She smiled to herself. She wondered how he would look at her if she asked for one of those non-alcoholic 'mocktails' they served to teetotallers? She'd never been much of a drinker, most alcohol gave her a headache, and during college she'd usually offered to be the designated driver if she'd gone out.

Maybe that was what Vander had liked about her. She'd often wondered because she'd certainly felt she'd let him down in some way, though he'd never said.

Nick glanced up, saw her skulking behind the pillar, and gestured her over. Well, maybe he wasn't totally disinterested.

She straightened away from the column and smiled shyly. Funny how that little tug in her stomach made her mouth curve. Her feet seemed pretty eager to move his way too and she tried not to wiggle like the last woman had.

He gestured to a stool at the side of the bar. 'Hello, there, Dr Tara. Fancy a drink?'

She smiled back. 'Non-alcoholic?'

'Sure.' He gestured to his makings. 'I'll have you know there is just as much skill needed for a really top mocktail, if not more.'

'You reckon you're pretty good at these, do you?'

'The best.'

'I see you lack in confidence.'

'I know. Sad really. How about a *No*-jito?' His white teeth flashed and she had to grin and the extraneous noises faded until it was as if the two of them were in a private little bubble. She bet all the girls behind her at the pool felt like that too. He went on to explain. 'Crushed mint, loads of limes, sugar syrup and soda?'

'Sounds great.' She shook off her absorption of him and glanced around. 'How's the bar-manager gig going?'

He smiled at the half-naked women on loungers spread out in a fan in front of him. 'Always fun.'

She shook her head sadly. 'Tsk, tsk. Men.'

He leaned towards her. 'Perhaps it should be *"Tsk tsk, women"*? Though I don't mean that. I love women. I have sisters I adore and a new girlfriend every month.'

Tara wondered if he was warning her. Temporary. Don't plan a wedding. Nice if he was. Because that suited her down to the ground!

Nick wondered if he was warning her. Bit of an exaggeration, that monthly girlfriend thing, but he certainly wasn't into permanence. Had discovered long ago that even the most likely couple would stretch to find eternal happy-ever-after. But to warn about his preference for the short term was not his usual tactic when he was trying to chat up a woman.

What made this one different? He'd kept an eye out for her but had been unexpectedly busy with his duties and he'd have much preferred it if his sister had decided on a position with less responsibilities.

Dr Tara had intruded into his thoughts persistently last night when the sea had played games. He'd bet there were a few seasick passengers and some crew not used to the sway of the ship yet. 'Did the swell bother you last night?'

'No.' She shrugged. 'I have a cast-iron stomach.' He pushed the peanuts her way but she wasn't interested. 'A few of the new beauty staff were a little queasy and we doled out some anti-emetics.'

Nick shoved the cheese and crackers across and she ignored them too. She glanced at the women and changed the subject away from medicine. 'What about your patrons?'

'It was pretty quiet for a second night.' Lord, he just wanted to feed her. He used his tongs to put two hulled strawberries in a dish in front of her. She couldn't miss them. To his delight she picked one up absently and bit into it. Gorgeous lips, white little teeth... Nick's stomach kicked as he tried not to mimic her.

He glanced at his watch for a bit of control. 'So, what time are you off duty?'

'Apart from being on call?' She patted her lips with a paper towel he gave her. 'I'm off now till lunch. Then off again at eight. Why?'

Maybe he shouldn't do this. He'd always listened to his instincts before so why was this so difficult? 'Care to join me for dinner about eight-thirty?'

She narrowed her eyes at him and then glanced away. 'I guess so.'

Had he sounded too eager? She certainly hadn't. But he'd seen a few other crew members eyeing her and it hadn't sat well with him. Another out-of-character trait she seemed to bring out in him. Maybe he just needed to demystify her attraction and then he'd understand what drew her to him.

# CHAPTER FOUR

AT TWENTY-THIRTY hours they sat in a quiet corner of the crew dining room, or middle mess as they called it, because it was common ground.

Nick was aware she'd normally eat in the first mess because that was where the officers congregated, and on this gig he ate with the auxiliary and admin staff.

The largest staff dining area catered for the seven hundred domestic and deckhand staff but there was always a little mix and match that went on with the dalliances.

It was after the usual time for dinner and before late supper so nobody came near them.

Unobtrusively Nick had been studying the fine veins in her hands. She was so frail when he really looked. There was that stupid protectiveness again. 'So what made you go to the Sudan?'

He pushed a bread stick her way but she ignored it. Two years? Nick was still flabbergasted. No wonder she looked like a strong wind would blow her over. One of his friends had lasted three months. He wanted to draw her into his arms and protect her. That was a serious worry. Apart from his sisters, he'd avoided the whole emotional responsibility thing.

'I went with my husband. We wanted to do something worthwhile, use our training, and after he died it was too hard to leave.'

The impact of her statement sat heavily in his chest. He wouldn't have picked her for a widow. There was a certain naive vulnerability he couldn't miss. 'I'm sorry. How did your husband die?'

She glanced away. 'Cholera.'

Ouch. 'Nasty.'

She looked back at him. 'Very.' Succinct.

'So why the Sudan?'

She shrugged. 'We'd both finished our internships and he met a midwife who'd worked in the displaced person refugee camps. She told him how they were crying out for GPs with obstetric training and he enquired. The next thing I knew we were there and I didn't lift my head up until a week ago when my boss said I needed to take a break.'

Nick shook his head. 'After two years. I'll bet.' He glanced at her hands again. She didn't wear a ring. Why was that? Almost ruminatively he said, 'What were they thinking of to leave you there so long?'

She blinked and for a horrible moment he thought she was going to cry and he wanted to kick himself. It brought home just how close to the edge she was and he vowed to himself he'd keep a close eye on her. Might even have a word to Wilhelm about her work hours.

'You don't want to talk about it?' He could see her squirming. He wanted her to eat something. He picked up the strawberry he'd kept for last and put it on her plate.

She shook her head. 'Not particularly.' But at least she absently ate the fruit. He was ridiculously relieved.

So she didn't want to talk about it. Good. Neither did he. Especially about her husband. 'Fine.'

She glanced away but he couldn't tell if she was upset from her voice when she spoke again.

Such a bright and cheery voice that said back off. 'Hey, I'm tougher than I look.' She turned to him and he decided her smile was only just forced. 'And here I am...' she spread her arms '...talking to a bar manager, on a ship cruising the Mediterranean, and very glad I don't have to think about anything disastrous.' She put down her fork.

'So, talk to me about something light and frivolous. That's why I'm cultivating you.'

So she was cultivating him, eh? Sounded promising and damn straight he could be frivolous. Well, he guessed that summed him up. Compared to her anyway.

It didn't seem the time to tell her he was a doctor too. Not frivolous enough. Or about his own transition through med school and rotation to learn the lot, anaesthetics, obstetrics and surgery. He'd had his moments requiring skill and dedication but compared to what he could imagine she'd been through, his world was a cinch.

Though frivolously speaking, he never had to get involved with patients and their real lives because he would only be there for a weekend or a month at the most because he was locum man.

So no talk of medicine and he told her what he thought she wanted to hear.

'I haven't been on a ship for a while but worked my way up from barman to cocktail master.' He puffed out his chest theatrically. 'Took out a medal at the world cocktail championships with a friend.'

He didn't usually tell people that, it had been years ago, but he guessed the title would sound playful enough for her, and he wanted to see that smile he knew was in there.

'So what do you do?'

'I mix drinks when the bar staff are on their breaks, make sure all the behind counter orders are filled and we don't run out of Margarita mix. I fill in when staff are sick and just try to keep everyone happy.' He shrugged. 'Apparently I'm pretty good at that.'

'I can see you are.' Now she smiled and it had been worth waiting for. He felt a flicker of satisfaction from lightening her mood and more than a flicker of awareness, as though the moon had just peeked through a bank of clouds outside. Bizarre how good she made him feel.

He leaned towards her and a tendril of hair fell across her face, making his finger itch to push it back. 'Been for a swim yet?' He fancied seeing her in a bikini.

'No. I'm very boring. Just getting used to things and finding my way around. I bet you use all the amenities.'

'Every single one.' He flashed his teeth at her and she smiled again. 'I like a good game of table tennis.'

'Do you? I used to have a very competitive streak for ball games.'

'Aha! That sounds like a challenge.'

Tara almost laughed out loud. The fizzing in her stomach was getting stronger. And was it all about a ball game? Was she challenging him?

Maybe she wasn't as bad at this as she'd thought she'd be. 'We'll see.'

He went on like a tour guide and she could feel herself relax more every minute. He was like her own personal cruise director. 'Then there's Movies Under The Stars, with deckchairs, checked blankets and popcorn, and of course the latest flicks.'

'Checked blankets, eh? Very observant for a man.'

He shrugged. 'My sisters have this thing for tablecloths under trees for picnics. So I have a soft spot for checks.'

The image of cuddling up with Nick and a blanket under Mediterranean stars was almost tangible. 'I'll watch out for those blankets.' Though she wasn't quite sure now just what she was watching out for.

'So why don't you let me show you around when we anchor off Naples? Maybe hire a convertible. We could take a drive down to Amalfi, check out Praiano and Positano.'

His chest tightened and he realised he was actually holding his breath. This was crazier by the minute. Her toffee gaze slid over his face thoughtfully and he could almost taste her sweetness. Something whispered sweet was dangerous.

'Sounds good. I've always wanted to see the Italian coastline from those windy roads.' She opened her eyes wide and he had an epiphany as to what they meant by 'almost fell in'. Was that a come-on? He sure as hell hoped so because he could feel his body stir like leaves in a breeze at that hint of promise.

'The roads have to be seen to be believed,' he warned with a grin. 'And they appeal to the frustrated Ferrari driver in me.'

'A Ferrari?' She pretended to frown. 'They must pay good wages where you work.'

He guessed he could hire one if he wanted to but he'd be too worried he'd scratch it. Not many cars were dent free on Italian roads. 'No. But maybe a little sports number so we can put the roof down.' He grinned. 'You know, feel the whoosh of air as the buses push us up against the cliff.' He watched her. Deliberately painting the picture to make sure she knew what she was getting into. To his delight, if anything her eyes sparkled more.

'Oh, yeah. I've heard about that. A little danger that's not blood-product related would be a great way to remember life is for living.'

Not blood-product related. He wanted to hug her. Felt the rapport. Medical people laughed at the oddest things and he was feeling a little more alive than usual himself.

Tara couldn't believe she was flirting like this. And had made an infectious-disease joke that he probably hadn't got. He might think she was loony but the idea of capturing a few hours of wind in her face and amazing views was enticing. Cathartic even. And she couldn't hide the fact the idea of spending time with someone light and mischievous like Nick wasn't a big plus too.

'So tell me about your morning,' Nick said. 'Any interesting cases?'

Did he really want to know? She doubted it. Probably the whole 'I'm paying attention to everything you say' persona he had down pat. 'It was fine. A few bouts of nausea and a fractured forearm.'

'They have an X-ray machine here, don't they?' Interest shone from his eyes and she enlarged slightly to explain.

'Yes.' She smiled at him for humouring her. 'Not something I've had to do personally before and interesting to learn how simple taking an X-ray really is. The patient's views are emailed away to a large centre to be reported on, and the results are emailed back.'

She shook her head, still bemused by the speed of reporting. 'Wilhelm had the results within two hours, which was even faster than my training hospital in Sydney.'

'Which hospital was that?' She saw his eyes sharpen and she frowned. Warning bells rang.

'In the south.' But she didn't go into more detail. She quite liked the fact he didn't know where she came from. 'A long way from here. But, of course, at the refugee camp we had nothing except our hands to decide if a bone was broken.'

She saw him accept she wasn't about to give out her home address and her relief expanded. She wasn't sure why she was so keen on keeping distance from the real world with him but it was better to err on the side of caution.

This whole Nick exercise was designed as a holiday flingette, just a tentative fling, and the

idea of the future or anything or anyone serious made her cringe. Like Saint Vitus's dance.
A full-body shudder. She knew for a fact she
wasn't mentally ready for any kind of normal
relationship.

'So the last two years will always have an impact on your work?'

Not just my work, she thought with sudden insight and a flash of her late husband's face. 'Of
course.' Images from their work flooded back,
some of them uplifting but most of them tragic,
and she winced. 'Another thing I don't want
to talk about. Tell me about the world cocktail
championships. I love the sound of that.' Blunt,
but she hoped, effective.

He studied her for a moment and saw him nod
with understanding but there was no way this
man would have any idea what she'd seen. 'You
mean the place where all the movers and shak-
ers go?'

Effective communication, then. She smiled. 'That would be the place.'

'Vegas.' He spread his arms. 'You gotta think big. And sparkly. We were dressed in black with blue sequins, my sisters had a ball making the outfits, and our drink was a Morrocan Marguarettaville.'

'Sounds deadly.' She couldn't keep the smile from her face and she was suddenly conscious of how big and handsome this man was. This man, who was paying intense attention to her. Quite a heady experience really for a girl from tent city.

He spread his hands self-deprecatingly. 'A cocktail that carries a decent kick. Made for slow sipping at sunset.'

The picture of the two of them sipping drinks on some beach seemed ridiculously easy to imagine. 'You'll have to make me one.' She laughed. 'One sunset when I can sleep in the next day.'

He put his finger to his lips and her gaze followed his finger. 'As long as you don't tell any-one the recipe.'

'My lips are sealed.' She'd said it and shouldn't have been surprised he glanced at her mouth in return. But she felt the heat.

For a woman who had minimal experience of seduction she had no trouble recognising his ability to turn it on.

Zap! Almost as if he'd touched her, and suddenly the making of drinks in competitions was ludicrously unimportant. His eyes darkened, his gaze locked on hers, the air thickened with his intention so that she knew he needed her alone, in the dark, locked in an embrace. And soon. Whoa, there. Her imagination was working over-time here.

Then he glanced down at the food they'd only picked at and she let out her breath. Felt like a fanciful idiot. 'Would you like to go outside? I'll share the rest while we walk. It's nice on deck at this time of night.'

Her stomach kicked. She hoped he hadn't read her mind again. He stood up and moved around to help pull out her chair and she stared at the tablecloth thoughtfully. He could be quite smooth at getting his own way when he wanted, but knowing it didn't stop her feet from shifting, standing, moving beside him with a little beat of anticipation fluttering in her throat.

When they stepped out onto the walkway around the ship he tucked her hand into his arm and after the initial shock she let her hand relax and just enjoyed the sensation of being close to a man she had to admit she fancied. She even had to fight down the heat in her cheeks like a schoolgirl. The concept made her grin. Her hip brushed his solid thigh as they walked and when they passed two female crew members walking together she even enjoyed the envious look they cast her.

A little devil of satisfaction made her fingers curl more tightly into his arm and his skin warmed her fingers. He must have felt her approval because he looked down at her and smiled.

She hurried into speech in case he read too much into her involuntary action. 'Maybe I could get used to forgetting the world on a cruise ship because it's all an illusion that only lasts twelve days.'

He tilted his head and studied her. 'Not everything is an illusion.'

That was a laugh. 'What's not an illusion?'

She watched him search for an example that was amusing and backed up her statement. This guy's life was an illusion. Which was why she liked him.

'I imagine the person with the broken arm is steeped in reality at the moment.'

She dug in her chin, refused to be deflected from her common-sense *aide memoire* that they had no future. Light, frivolous, she reminded herself again. 'I prescribed decent analgesia. Checked the cast wasn't too tight. I'd say she's floating along quite nicely despite it.'

She felt his glance brush over her again, felt it physically because her skin prickled, and she hurried into speech. 'You were going to tell how you became the world cocktail champion.'

'Well, I boasted a little. There were two of us. And we had an idea for a drink that resembled a boat and tasted like an island. To be sipped, as I said, at sunset.' He grinned. 'Lots of rum.'

He stopped beside a little tuck in the deck that created an alcove and she stopped beside him. The waves were quietly relentless, insistently slapping the side of the ship as the big white hull sliced its way through the swell. The breeze was cool and laden with the tang of salt as they sped to their next port.

At the bow of the ship, to the side, the wheelhouse hung out over the sea and she could just discern figures on duty.

They both turned to look out over the ocean as they leant on the cool lacquered rail and the intensity of the moment that had sprung from nowhere eased. The tension she'd picked up slowly dissipated from her neck as, in the distance, tiny flickers of light twinkled on the horizon from the nearest land.

'Gotta love the Italian coastline.' His hand swept along the land mass.

'Where do you think that is?'

He shrugged. 'There's so many cliff hewn townships plastered onto the side of Italy, I'd be guessing.' Then he moved his hip until it was firm alongside hers and she forgot the lights as his solid thigh imparted insidious heat like a warm current through a cold sea.

The slow slide of awareness seeped up her body until she couldn't resist her own lean to increase the pressure.

His hand tightened on hers and slowly but surely he drew her into his arms.

Nick's head bent closer, close but not all the way, and his voice rumbled in her ear. 'I'd really like to kiss you.'

It wasn't a question but it wasn't a demand either. Just a statement of how he felt and one she could wholeheartedly agree with.

She could do this—be brave enough to say what she'd been thinking, out loud. 'I think that would be nice.'

A flash of teeth in the dimness at her less than smooth answer but the result was good. His head bent and his mouth came down to stop just a breath away from hers until she leaned in and made the link. He returned with a gentle brush of those gorgeous lips that pressed against her mouth with a little fizz of connection she hadn't expected.

She'd actually assumed it was going to be hard work to learn to kiss again, not that she'd ever been remarkably good at it before, because there hadn't been much of it, but lessons and ratings and thoughts of her own ability seemed to slip away from her consciousness, like trying to catch the breeze in her fingertips.

Drifting into sensation.

Drifting into Nick. Nick's mouth, his breath mingled with hers, the wash of the waves against the side of the ship a distant accompaniment to the feel of his mouth moving over hers.

Then the slide of his other hand as he sought and found her free fingers and linked with them too. Dimly she admitted she liked that bond, just their mouths and their fingers joined and her breasts firm against his solid chest.

When his tongue touched hers gently she inhaled sharply and unconsciously flattened herself against him to deepen the sensation until unexpectedly she was lost to time and place and everything except the silent mating of mouths in this corner of the deck under the moonlight.

She'd never offered herself like this before or maybe she had offered but had never shared as an equal—been a part of the experience instead of the outsider not meeting some rigorous standard. The thought drifted. She winced at the disloyalty that still bit but, boy, imagine if it had been Vander missing the ingredients, not her. Heretic thought.

But there was no doubt this man ignited a slow burn inside her that she'd never expected so that she could feel herself almost glow incandescently.

'Stop thinking,' she murmured to herself against his mouth.

He said, 'Mmm' back, and suddenly it wasn't so hard to let go of all thought, revel in the moment, explore it, until dimly she realised he was moving backwards, drawing away, squeezing her fingers downwards as if to help her return her feet to the deck.

'Oh, my.' Tara stood back and compressed her lips as she slowly withdrew her fingers from his. 'Oh, my,' she said again, and he pulled her into his chest until her face was pressed against his shirt and his mouth rested on her hair. She could feel the thumping away under her cheek and there was no doubt his heart rate had picked up. So he wasn't immune either.

Nick squeezed her for a moment, they both sighed, and he spoke into her hair. 'I think you'd better go to bed.'

She stepped back, cast one glance into his unsmiling face and turned, pretending her heart wasn't thumping like the ship's engines below her feet.

She walked away. Oh, my. What the heck had happened there? One kiss. Or a series of kisses that had made her head spin.

She put her hand out for the rail and used it as a support to get her back to the doorway that led inside. She could feel her lips tingling and when the ocean breeze caught her hair and spread it across her face she couldn't help touching her mouth as she dragged it away. Apart from being sensitive, her lips felt no different—she couldn't say the same for the thumping in her chest. Either the guy was seriously charismatic or she was seriously at risk of being a pushover. Not what she'd planned.

Nick watched her go and he inhaled a big breath in through his nose as he tried to quieten the boys in the basement, who'd wanted to break out and conquer. It had been let go then or who knew where they'd end up? And this he didn't want to rush.

Since when? Innocence causing his undoing? And why did her untrained mouth seem more erotic than the most practised women he'd been with while her fluttering fingers left trails on his skin that still glowed with angel dust? He rubbed his hands over his arms as if to break her spell as he took another breath.

He could still sense her perfume. Nothing he'd come across before—violets? Tara was like a violet. Hiding at the side of life, doing her job, easily bruised, overshadowed by the showy roses yet surprisingly beautiful when you took the time to look.

She wore a top note of spring that blended with her warm skin like the kiss of an angel and complemented her lack of artifice. A little old-fashioned. Like he wanted to be when he held her. Whoa.

Stop! He had good reasons why he wanted to keep his relationships super-casual. He did not want to be another man who broke Tara's heart. Even in the brief mention she'd made of her departed husband he'd sensed it had been a less than perfect marriage. She deserved a good man, not a good-time guy like him.

Nick took off for the crew's mess and hopefully some diversion at a sharp pace. Maybe find a woman he could chat up and go dancing with. Someone who was here for the fun to take his mind off what he really wanted to do. Like search out a certain young medic and lose himself despite the danger?

# CHAPTER FIVE

WHEN Tara woke two days later their cruise had docked at Naples and she decided she liked this business of going to bed in one city and waking in the next. There were even a few inklings she could settle into the routine of the ship's obsession with the clock. Begin to enjoy this slice of time that didn't belong to the real world.

Her shore day as a tourist promised the first frivolous—there was that word again—excitement in a long while. She couldn't help the little jump in her pulse rate at the thought of spending the day with the heady cocktail that was Nick.

The feeling was amplified by the fact she hadn't seen him at all during the preceding twenty-four hours despite several attempts during her breaks to nonchalantly pass the Casablanca bar.

Where had this light-hearted woman come from? She couldn't believe only a few days ago she'd been working under primitive conditions in a tent city of eighty thousand people with round-the-clock disasters.

Sickeningly, her mood plunged and she dragged herself back from the abyss with a determination borne of need, to another world, a different world she was only just discovering, the here and now of lighter responsibility.

Focus on yesterday where her work in the ship's medical centre was like a walk in the park compared to the Sudan. And the best thing was she couldn't lose a baby or a mother because the rules for travel on board excluded women over twenty weeks pregnant and infants less than six months old.

Non-critical diagnostics that required routine action were a breeze. They'd had two crew members with unexplained high temperatures, whom they'd isolated and were transferring off the ship today, and a few muscle strains and headaches, but apart from that the staff seemed a healthy lot.

Wilhelm had been a little busier with a series of minor complaints and two asthmatic children. Gwen had brought Tommy back with a temperature, which had settled with paracetamol.

The most serious case had been the dehydrated woman with deep-vein thrombosis who'd needed heparin and transfer.

Tara was so well used to finding venous access in very ill women she had no trouble at all when asked to help out. The hardest part was not to keep comparing the patient load to the last two years.

But that was work and today was play.

Most of the passengers would be off on shore tours and Wilhelm had assured her she could have the whole day free as long as they were back by six-thirty before the ship sailed.

The anticipation built as she walked sedately down the stairs to the disembarkation deck in her new blue T-shirt she'd bought from the on-board boutique.

Nick looked especially debonair in an open-necked white shirt and fawn shorts, his strong legs deeply tanned all the way down to his sandalled feet. He waited for her in front of the gang-way and they swiped their crew cards to record their absence.

Security waved them on with a grin and suddenly she was on solid ground. Just the two of them.

The tarmac of the pier shifted unexpectedly under her feet and she wobbled a little.

Nick laughed and put out a hand. 'You just need your land legs.'

The ground steadied and he let go to retrieve the keys from the attendant.

Tara hesitated before she started walking again.

Maybe she was still unsteady or maybe it was realising she was suddenly on her own and getting into a little red sports car with a man she barely knew.

Nick must have noticed her falter because he stopped and looked as he held open her door to the rental car that waited on the pier for them. 'You okay?'

She didn't say anything, couldn't actually, was just having a private little panic attack about why he'd possibly want to spend time with her. She had no social skills, was skin and bone and downright boring. She conveniently forgot it had been Nick who'd asked her along.

He let go of the doorhandle and put his hand over his heart. 'It's okay. We'll have fun.' He shrugged. 'Just reminding you, while I don't have a written reference, we have to work together on the ship. You know in my other life I have sisters

I adore and can promise have never frightened a woman in my life.'

It wasn't because she was scared. Tara mentally shook herself. He'd asked her. If they didn't prove compatible there'd be tons of gorgeous scenery to ease the conversational burden. And she doubted making conversation was a problem Nick had any issues with.

She didn't know why she was having cold feet, unless it was because she was more worried they'd be too compatible. And that was ridiculous.

Nick noted the tension in her face. So he wasn't the only one unsure if they were playing with fire. Though he doubted she had enough experience to know what it was she was feeling nervous about.

She shook her head, more at herself than at him. 'Sorry. Just out of practice.'

He cursed himself. He'd suspected she was

fragile and still he'd gone steaming in like a bozo on steroids.

'It's me who should apologise. I did railroad you into this.' And shouldn't have if he'd had any sense, but it was too late now.

He glanced towards the city. 'If you like, we can just drive into town, have a coffee and come back. I didn't think you needed Pompeii today so wasn't going here. Though we could zip up to the top of Vesuvius and admire the bay. It's spectacular from up there. We don't have to make a day of it. I keep forgetting you'll still be tired from your work.'

She lifted her pretty little chin. 'I'm fine. Let's go.'

Yes! He'd offered and she'd declined. The relief was ridiculous. He told himself he wasn't suddenly feeling like he'd won the lottery. That was just because he was looking forward to taking the car for a spin. Any company would have been good.

An hour later, on the cliff road coming into Amalfi, Tara wasn't so sure she was cut out for this type of excitement.

'How can you drive here?' Tara's fingers whitened unobtrusively as she gripped the edge of the seat beside her leg and tried not to look at the rocks in the ocean below.

When he took his eyes off the tarmac to smile her way she gripped tighter. 'For goodness' sake, keep your eyes on the road.'

Nick laughed but complied. 'I have an aunt who owns a hotel in Praiano, a little town on the cliff between Amalfi and Positano. We used to come down here for holidays. Learnt to drive on motorbikes here and progressed to cars.'

He didn't sound Italian. 'So you grew up in Italy?'

'Between here and Sydney. My mum was Italian and moved to Australia when she married my dad. We spent a lot of holidays here.' He grinned at her quickly then returned his attention back to the road.

Tara frowned. It all sounded very breezy and humorous but there was something underlying that suggested to Tara it hadn't been as smoothly transitional as he made out.

Another scooter with a death-wish pillion passenger slipped between them, a bus and the sheer drop to the ocean five hundred feet below. She let the subject drop. 'Those guys are crazy!'

He flashed his teeth and dared her to live dangerously. Somehow it was infectious. She'd wanted to know she was alive. Her fingers loosened. What the heck. Hanging on wouldn't save her anyway. She grinned back with determination. She was going to enjoy today. If it killed her. 'Do your worst, then.'

They scooted down the mountain, zipping

around coaches as incredibly skilled bus drivers pulled over to stop the backlog of cars and the cheeky motorcycles ran around both of them.

To the side, the cliff fell sheer to the sea hundreds of feet below, and on the azure water cruise ships dotted the horizon while charter boats left trails of whitewash across the ocean.

They coiled their way into Amalfi and the vibrancy of the little Italian seaside town made Tara's eyes widen and her breath ease out in a sigh. 'It's so pretty. And look at the shops!'

Her eyes flicked between gaily decorated windows like an addict in a chocolate factory and she frowned at herself. 'Do you know how long it is since I saw shops like these?'

Pretty dresses fluttered on hangers outside doorways and she could feel herself lean towards them. She was so shallow. How materialistic could you get? Apart from her new T-shirt it had been years since she'd bought clothes. Vander had been very scornful of fashion. 'They make me feel guilty. An indulgence when so many people don't have food.'

Nick sniffed. 'As Kiki, my youngest sister, would say, piffle!' He pulled into a tiny parking spot as if their bumper bar wasn't less than an inch from the car in front and she shook her head incredulously.

'How on earth did you do that?'

He shrugged. 'Parking in Italy is an art form. Not much car space so use it to the max.' He turned to face her. 'As for not buying clothes, guilt is self-indulgent—so you may as well use real self-indulgence and go shopping.'

She wrinkled her forehead as she replayed his words in her head. How could guilt be self-indulgent? Was she wallowing in it? She didn't think so but maybe she could shop a little, try the experience out, and see how it went. 'You'll be sorry. I feel like I could hunt bargains all day.'

He waggled his brows. 'Do your worst. I'm an experienced bag carrier.'

She blinked. Didn't shopping made men frown? 'You sure? You could meet me at a bar.'

He grinned. 'I really do enjoy watching women disappear into change rooms and twirl and frown and dither.' He shrugged. 'Sick, I know, but it amuses me.'

She glanced longingly at the fluttering frocks and scarves. 'A little walk around wouldn't hurt.'

He glanced up the street, found what he was looking for and drew her forward. 'Try this one. My sisters come here all the time and there's a chair for me to enjoy the show.'

She shrugged, happy to be steered, and Nick watched her disappear into the shop before he followed at a leisurely pace. When Tara had slipped into the little change room Nick engaged the owner in conversation, and when Tara came out without finding anything she really liked Nick stood up and handed her a new selection.

'The saleslady suggested these with your colouring.' He watched the confusion in her face as she warred with the idea he'd actually selected clothes for her and the fact that she'd already been in there ten minutes.

He sat down again in the chair and raised his bottle of water. 'Go.' She glanced at her watch and dithered. He could see she wanted to try more.

He grinned at her. 'And this time can I please see the ones you fancy?' He held out his hands. 'Not bored. Honest!'

Watching Tara was as enjoyable as he'd imagined once she started to venture out with each new outfit.

Shy, face pink, she did the fastest twirl in history when he gestured for her to show him the back, with a quick glance at his face to see if he thought she looked okay. This was the part he loved about women. Nick could feel it expand in his chest. See her confidence grow as each new outfit appeared. Loved the little frown when she disagreed with his verdict.

An hour later Tara was over it. Nick could have spent the day watching, but hoarded the bags and seemed to find a new delight in every corner of the shop for her to try. Already she had three dresses, three shorts and shirt sets, and two new bikinis she hadn't let him see. 'Enough,' she said.

He dropped his lip. 'Shame,' he replied, then grinned. 'But fine. We'll put these in the boot and take a run up to Praiano to my aunt's hotel for lunch. The view from there's incredible.'

He opened the door to their zippy little sports car and as she bent to climb in she caught a woman watching her enviously from the side of the road. Her face warmed as Nick stowed the bags in the back. Tara felt like shaking her head but then realised she really was living a fun life. She just needed to remember not to apologise for it.

Consciously she relaxed her hands and lifted her face to the breeze. As they took off she reminded herself this leg also involved another hair-raising ride along the coast road but she did trust Nick's driving to get them there safely. They'd be fine.

Fifteen minutes later they zoomed into the cliff-hugging town of Praiano, where finally Nick pulled in front of the white facade of a hotel.

Tara read the sign: 'Hotel Tramonto d'Oro'. A bus squeezed past and she wondered why a hotel would be built so close to the road.

As soon as they stepped inside the foyer she could see the vista that stretched right across the cerulean sea. 'Well, that explains it,' she murmured as her nose itched to press up against the glass on the other side of the room. Before she could move to the windows a stylish Italian woman appeared from the office and swooped on Nick.

'Nico!' She glanced at Tara and smiled. 'So my nephew has brought you to see me.' She glanced at them both and threw her hands into the air with Gallic drama. 'So finally he has fallen in love.'

Tara blushed and shook her head. 'No.' Good grief, no. 'We're just friends.'

Nick sent her an apologetic look but appeared unperturbed while Tara wanted to crawl under one of the big plush lounges in front of the window and hide.

In Italian Nick did his own gesticulating until his aunt laughed. '*Sì, sì.* Just friends.' She laughed again. 'But you are hungry? No?'

Tara lifted her head as her stomach rumbled. She could answer that one. '*Sì.*'

'Then you shall have the best table. The view is good today. No haze.'

Angelica shooed them in front of her and Tara's mouth opened at the view across the Mediterranean Sea from the lounges. A gelato-hued town in the distance hung on the cliffs like different flavours in an ice-cream shop and island smudges dotted the expanse into the distance.

When they sat at a wrought-iron table on the long outside veranda Tara couldn't drag her eyes from the vista. 'I can't believe I didn't bring a camera.'

'Neither can I.' But Nick wasn't looking over the rail as he spoke.

She pointed to the postcard village in the distance. 'So is that Positano?'

'Yep. Pretty place, great shops.' He didn't glance at it. Just watched her as if trying to work something out that puzzled him. Tara screwed up her face at him. 'Stop it.'

He blinked, shook his head and turned his attention to the seascape. 'Sorry. I was somewhere else.'

Just the sort of thing Vander would say. She winced. Well, that wasn't very flattering, she thought perversely, and now she wished he'd look at her again. How contrary could you get? She'd never been any good at this girl-boy thing.

Nick's mind surely was somewhere else. Vivid visions of some of the activities they could do there, like get a room, spend the day there, distracted him and he glanced down at the menu and tried to concentrate. 'We'll go down to Positano after lunch and maybe catch a ferry across to Capri. It's a beautiful trip. Or at least see some boats come in if we run out of time.'

Her beautiful eyes narrowed and he knew, no idea how, what she was thinking. Conscientious and paranoid they'd be late back. She'd brought it up on the car already on the way here. He wished he hadn't mentioned the word 'late'.

'What time do we need to leave?'

'Relax if you can.' He put his hand over her hers and squeezed it. She tensed and he smiled ruefully. Well, that hadn't worked. 'I'm a responsible guy and I'd want to be back in Amalfi by three to give us enough leeway. I get the impression you don't want to miss the ship on our first shore excursion.'

Her eyes widened with distress and he cursed himself for his flip reply.

'There's no chance of that, is there?' She began to look seriously worried and he backpedalled to make up lost ground.

He'd never been so conscious of a woman's moods. So concerned that she would worry. 'We'll give ourselves loads of time.'

She glanced at her watch again and he lifted

his hand and pressed her arm back to the table. 'It's okay. Enjoy the view. Life is short.'

'Family saying?'

'My saying.'

Tara drew a breath and forced her eyes to the horizon. Once there it was hard to look away. She really needed to stop being so tense. Nick had done all this before and she was supposed to be having F.U.N.

She savoured the calamari, adored the insalata Caprese, and sipped a limoncello, the lemon liqueur made by Nick's uncle from their own lemon orchard. By the time they'd finished their lunch and waved goodbye to Nick's aunt she was feeling much more relaxed.

So relaxed that she didn't even blink when they proceeded past cliff-hugging mansions and through mountain tunnels and over bridges with pylons planted hundreds of feet below in the rock. At last they drove down the mountain into the postcard-perfect Positano with its colourful buildings and deckchair-strewn beaches.

The shops were even more enticing than those in Amalfi but Tara was eager to swim in the salty Mediterranean. Cool her cheeks and her thoughts because Nick was making her smile and laugh more than she could remember ever smiling and laughing.

Nick decided the day was going well and was looking ahead to the new bikini he hadn't been allowed to see, but he didn't say that to Tara. Instead he indulged her, hired a change shed, and waited with bated breath for her to reappear.

# CHAPTER SIX

Nick whistled. It had been worth the wait.

Tara tugged at the side of the bikini bra as she opened the door of the change shed and Nick chewed hard on his lip so he didn't smile.

'I think I must have picked up the wrong one. Is this bikini too small?' Tugging the sides did incredible things to the front of the small scrap of material but he wasn't saying anything that would jeopardise the beauty of the moment.

'No. It's fine.' He forced himself to turn and glance at the inviting blue of the Mediterranean. He'd need a cool shower soon if they didn't get in. 'Looks good. Ready?'

He risked another look. A tiny, unconvinced frown marred her brow, but as far as he was concerned she looked hot. Maybe too hot. He glanced around to see who else was looking. The fact that she could do with a few more pounds just made him want to hug her more. She still did a delightful job of filling out the swimwear.

Tara tugged again at the edge of the bra cup and Nick smiled at her. 'Leave it. You look gorgeous. Now, come into the water before I have to carry you in there just so I can get my hands on you.'

She froze, glanced at him, and to his relief began to giggle. He decided she had a seriously cute laugh. 'I won't need you. I hear the water round here is especially buoyant.'

He enjoyed the view some more and decided now was the time to submerge. Once in the water he felt way more relaxed and the angle was good for watching Tara edge in gingerly across the pebbles.

'Don't they have sand at the beach in Italy?'

He grinned. 'Lots of volcanoes make lots of pebbled beaches.'

She sank under the water on her back. As she took the weight off her feet and savoured the coolness of the water he watched her lips part in a blissful sigh and tried not to stare at her breasts poking up. 'Oh, my.'

He remembered the last time she'd said that. He sank lower in the water. Her little feet floated to the surface and she lay there suspended without effort.

Her eyes shut. 'This is so cool.'

'You mean the temperature or the fact that you can float without trying?'

'Both.' She sighed again and drifted with her lashes on her cheeks, which meant he could drink in the sight of her to his heart's content. 'The sea is glorious. To think I've watched it for days and I've only just touched it.'

Nick drifted closer until he could brush her hand. 'Hmm. I feel the same.'

She opened her eyes lazily and paddled with her hands until she bumped into his chest. 'Oops. Sorry.'

'Don't be.' His hands captured her shoulders and pulled her slowly into his chest so that she was anchored on his lap in the water. 'I'm a sea god. You have to pay a tax when you bump into me.'

She closed one eye. 'Well, I'm a mermaid. Do you have any idea how dangerous I am?'

Oh, yes. She was dangerous all right, much more than a woman who knew the rules, but he still turned her to face him.

'I laugh at danger,' he said, and she giggled again.

So he kissed her, which was what he'd wanted to do since she'd met him at the gangplank this morning. Time stood still and her skin felt like silk under the water as she twined her arms around his neck.

When she returned his kiss with such an innocent ardour it tore at his heart and tightened his chest. He couldn't remember when it had been like this. Holding Tara was precious, yet terrifying, and some of that fear was residual warning of becoming too fond of someone.

Of the risks that he didn't take or believe in. His friends would roll around on the floor at the suave Nick mentally sweating like a nervous teenager at where to put his hands.

The kiss dissolved into a hot and lustful memory and she snuggled into him with ridiculous faith that she was safe, and he felt his chest swell at her trust. He vowed to earn it, though he wasn't sure why this was a necessary part now when it wasn't usually, and he worried at the thought of the one tiny untruth between them.

His fingers, of their own volition, began to gently knead her shoulders, gently massage her neck and the tightness within. To his further discomfort the slide of his hand across her skin was torture, especially when she purred and stretched under his fingers like a satisfied kitten.

He felt his lips curve with the warmth of satisfaction as knots softened and dissolved the more he stroked until he closed his eyes, stroking her by an unknown instinct, time forgotten, and she was soft as liquid in his arms, as if they had both become one with the waves lapping against them.

'Mmm. Your skin.'

He dropped a kiss and she sighed into him just as a family arrived to swim.

They both opened their eyes, saw the tiny baby cradled in his father's arms, helpless and mewling, and she stiffened in his arms. He felt the tension soak into her like ink into chalk as she slid out of his arms.

When she turned to face him, despite the smile on her face, the darkness of memories in her eyes made him want to hug her to him but she didn't give him the chance.

'I think I'll get out. Let's go down to the wharf, see the ferries come in. And I want to look at one of those shops I saw that only sell white clothes.'

That forced bright voice and a protective wall back in place around her was so high and strong he knew he wasn't getting back in there for a while.

'Sure.' He stood up and faced the shore. 'Maybe we'll manage one more swim before we go.'

'You're on.' She waded from the water and he watched her tread gingerly across the pebbled beach.

He wished. But he'd rally and maybe that was half the draw. Capturing and connecting with a reluctant mermaid. He tried not to listen to the warning voice that wondered if it was more than that.

In the end the afternoon passed as a series of cameo moments of a beautiful woman and gorgeous surroundings and lots of promise. Nick didn't want it to end but he knew it had to.

Tara kept going back in her mind to that drugged relaxation when Nick had massaged her shoulders in the water. His gentle strength had miraculously soothed months of neck tension and shoulder aches and there in the water she'd felt like she'd stepped into a fantasy resort with her very own gigolo.

Before she'd seen the baby. The sight should have made her smile, any normal woman would have, but, no, she had plunged back into darkness, it had all come back and she wondered if the memories would ever go so she could be the sort of woman a man would want to stay with.

She glanced to the horizon where islands were

dotted below the blue sky and the day was drawing to an end. For the last few hours she'd almost banished the last of the spectres that had tried to ruin her morning with Nick.

Briefly reality surfaced as they sat next to each other on sun loungers and she said, 'You sure we have enough time to get back to the ship?'

'Tons.'

Tara sighed and rested back in the chair. She did trust him. 'If you say so.'

Two hours later Tara glanced anxiously at her watch as they slowed to a halt. This was taking too long. She didn't care how much fun they'd had or how beautiful the beaches were. She'd never been late for work in her life, responsible doctors weren't, and she'd bet this irresponsible cocktail waiter thrived on it.

Nick could feel the waves of distress beating across the space between them in the car like heat waves across the sand they'd not long left. He had factored in extra time but obviously something was up as they rolled to a stop.

Because of the winding road he couldn't tell if the trouble was a hundred yards ahead or ten miles.

He pulled on the handbrake and turned to face her. After a second of observation he lowered his voice in the face of her turmoil. 'I'm just going to talk to the bus driver behind us. He'll have spoken to other drivers on his mobile and might know why we've stopped.'

She nodded and turned to look out her window. Nick winced and opened his door. She was such a serious little thing and he hoped they did make it back in time because he doubted she'd trust him in a hurry again if he let her down here.

*'Buon giorno,'* he said as he leant against the side of the bus at the driver's window. After

a thirty-second conversation he nodded and sprinted back to the car.

'A motorcyclist and his girlfriend have come off his bike around the next corner. Come on. We're needed.'

He saw her swallow. 'Oh. A young woman?'

He saw the panic before she clamped down on it, glanced ahead and then back. 'Look. You don't have to come. Seriously. They'd have it in hand and I can do the muscle bits.'

Not the right thing to say because he saw her stiffen her shoulders. 'Don't be ridiculous. Of course a doctor can help. At least I'm used to dealing without equipment.'

Tara pushed back the dread that had hit her out of nowhere. She'd let herself relax today. Let down her guard. Fool. Of course death and disaster followed her. Now she needed to kick herself into gear and do what she always did. Toughen up. Cope. Work. Save.

The heat beat off the black tarmac of the road as she rounded the bend and the first thing she saw was the wheel of the motorbike poking out from under the bus.

As she walked swiftly towards it she could make out the pale faces of the passengers staring out the window and in some distant space in her mind she hoped none of them had a heart condition.

But her eyes were on the girl and suddenly she was back in the Sudan. The tang of blood thick in the air, the beat of fear and shock and urgency from those around, and over all the slowing of time as someone's life drained away.

The young woman lay on her back on a spine board ready to move to the waiting ambulance with her rounded belly pointing to the sky and her pretty white shirt damply crimson.

For a second Tara's mind recoiled at the farce

she would be safe from losing mothers and babies.

The young woman's terrified eyes were fixed on the anxious female ambulance officer who bent over her as she attempted to tape a line for urgent replacement fluids.

Tara crossed swiftly with Nick beside her and they spoke simultaneously. 'Pregnant. Tilt the uterus.'

They looked at each other and Nick broke into Italian as they bent down, and as soon as the paramedic understood, Tara supported the neck brace as Nick and the paramedic tilted the board to shift the weight of the heavy uterus to the side off the young woman's major blood vessels.

As they repositioned the woman he explained to the paramedic that while on her back the weight of the baby would be dangerously slowing the mother's reduced blood flow to her heart and brain. The woman's thin backpack was beside her and he packed it in under the board on the right side as Tara supported her, but just as they did so their patient gasped once and then her eyes glazed.

Tara blinked. She'd seen this too many times when a heart stopped, and unless they could give a huge transfusion this woman and her baby would die, regardless of how good the bag ventilation and cardiac massage the paramedics had begun was.

She'd performed too many of these crash Caesareans over the last two years at cardiac arrest but the concept remained the same. Thirty per cent of the injured mother's blood volume was being diverted to the placenta and the baby and was taking from her vital organs. With not enough blood to go around, they would both die. They had four minutes for the baby without maternal circulation.

She snapped the order at Nick. 'Find a scalpel

and big sponges in case they can't get her heart going in time. And get people here to face the other way and form a human screen.' She turned back and began to open the buttons to the woman's chest around the working paramedics until Nick could return, and she prayed she wouldn't have to do what was rapidly becoming the patient's last hope.

Nick understood immediately. He knew of doctors who had been faced with difficult decisions and had acted. He admired them. Once he might have been one, but not now. Caesarean on a dead or dying woman. No theatre operating staff or sterile conditions. But who cared about germs if the patient was dead? Infection could be treated later—death couldn't.

No anaesthetic but, then, the woman was deeply unconscious, technically dead as her heart wasn't beating by itself from the lack of blood.

Which ironically helped with blood loss from the splash-and-slash surgery.

The most direct route to the baby was down the midline of the mother, scoop baby out before it too died from lack of circulation, pack the uterus with sponges to stop bleeding and resume cardiac massage more efficiently with the patient now flat on her back again.

Great theory if you had the courage, Nick thought savagely as he fired orders at the paramedics. Why couldn't he speak up and tell Tara he knew what she was thinking and it was a good idea?

He flicked his medical identification, and hurried back to Tara with the minimal equipment. Brave strategy—but he'd never seen a good outcome. She didn't let that frighten her. He thrust sterile gloves at her. 'Please put the gloves on.'

'Don't worry. Where I've been working we're very careful about protection.' She donned them swiftly and took the scalpel. He saw her close her eyes briefly and then she opened them and narrowed her gaze.

Nick watched in awe as the fastest and boldest operative retrieval he'd ever seen in his life was performed by this slip of a woman he hadn't realised possessed such single-minded determination.

'Nearly there. Are you right with the baby?' she said tersely.

He'd have to be. He wouldn't let her down. Tara clamped and cut the cord and Nick held out his gloved hands covered by a small rug retrieved from the ambulance.

The baby girl was white and floppy and Nick took her and rubbed her little face and chest, and to his delight she whimpered feebly and even began to flex her legs weakly as he placed the small resus bag over her tiny mouth and nose.

He puffed three breaths from the bag through the mask and watched the little chest rise.

Incredibly the baby began to cry, then with increasing loudness she wailed, and Nick felt the sting of unfamiliar tears burn in his throat. He hadn't even cried when his parents had died.

He looked across at Tara and they shared a searing moment of joint relief before Tara turned back to the mother. In some corner of his mind he wouldn't have been surprised to see tears in Tara's eyes but there were none. Her face stayed frozen with determination to save this woman.

'Baby's okay,' he said unnecessarily, and then a bossy grandmother pushed through the throng. 'Give to me. I am nurse. Save the mother.'

Nick nodded, handed the squirming baby over to competent arms and turned back to Tara. 'Removing tilt now.' Then he changed places with the flagging paramedic, who'd been doing cardiac massage grimly throughout the operation, her stunned eyes incredulously trying not to watch the macabre events.

'I've found the torn femoral artery and I'm tying it off now,' Tara said. 'They can fix it later.'

Within a minute, with the mother's blood supply now bypassing the uterus, there was enough blood to fill her heart's chambers and help the cardiac massage achieve its goal of restarting the heart.

Nick saw the flicker of a beat in her neck and the paramedic listened quickly with the stethoscope and nodded. 'Got a pulse,' Nick said to Tara.

Tara sank back as she packed the wound with the last sponge. 'Right. Let's load and go. They can stitch her up at the hospital if she makes it.' She glanced at Nick, still totally focused. 'I'll go with her—you follow.'

Nick looked then he nodded. One of them had

to go and Tara needed to see this through, but he'd be there for her at the door of the hospital.

All the way there as he followed the ambulance his heart beat with post-adrenalin rush and a sizzle of pride in Tara. She'd been amazing. Incredible. He'd never forget her slight body performing rapid surgery under the most primitive conditions.

Her actions shook his conception of self. Would he have coped as well if he'd had to call it?

Should he be out there learning more and not coasting like he was? Avoiding the difficult decisions by flying in and out. Doing stints on cruise ships. Sure, he stepped into different short-staffed situations and managed to be the one they wanted back next time, but he hadn't stretched himself like Tara had stretched herself.

Early in his career, not long after his parents had died, the one time he'd become involved and stuck his neck out, he'd almost left it too late.

Told himself his suspicions were ungrounded, because the truth was too horrific for a playboy to grasp, and had almost caused the death of a child. Since then he'd shied away from responsibility because he still hadn't forgiven himself for that. Didn't deserve forgiveness.

But Tara made him want to be more and he'd never felt that before today. Never considered forgiving himself and stepping up to the plate again.

An hour later, he met her at the entry to Emergency and helped her climb wearily into their hire car. He closed her door and walked swiftly around to the other side. When he was back at the wheel he looked across and her thick lashes were resting on her cheeks again but in repose it was a different face from the one in the water that day.

Lines of strain and dark shadows under her eyes proclaimed the toll that had been taken. 'You okay?'

Her lashes lifted. 'A day with a difference.' She sighed and then grimaced. 'But then again not very different from last week.'

Nick turned the key in the ignition. 'When I spoke to the nurse she said the baby is perfect. Mum is still critical.'

She made no move to do up her seat belt and Nick glanced at her unfocused gaze as she stared at the ambulances parked in front of them. He leaned across and buckled her belt.

'You did well, Tara. We'll be back at the ship soon.' She did that blinking thing with her eyes that he was beginning to recognise was Tara marshalling her thoughts, cute in a getting-to-know-her kind of way, and turned her head to face him.

'So were you. Amazing.' She shook her head, then frowned as if she was trying to work out what niggled. 'Too amazing?'

It certainly wasn't the time now for coming

clean. 'I wasn't the one who did a crash Caesarean on the side of the road.'

She winced. 'Another memory to add to the batch—but I must admit I've done a few in my time.' She sighed. 'I just want to sleep now the panic is over.'

'Then sleep. We won't be back at the ship for an hour or more. Plenty of time for a nap.'

'That's not very polite of me.' She almost smiled. 'Were we on a date or was that in another century?'

'Any of my dates who do surgery while we're out is allowed to rest. Close your eyes.'

So she did but Tara had no thought that she would really go to sleep.

When she woke up her mouth was dry and she hoped to heck she hadn't been dribbling because her neck was cricked from drooping.

Nick pulled onto the wharf and to her relief the ship was still there. They hadn't missed it but suddenly it wasn't so overwhelmingly important. But maybe she'd think twice before she rushed to go on a car tour again.

Nick opened her door and helped her out before he handed the keys over to a young man who'd hurried over. One of the officers at the bottom of the gangway waved to hurry them up.

Tara quickened her pace. 'Will we get into trouble for being late?'

Nick smiled. 'I think the excuse makes up for it.'

Still she frowned. 'I should see Wilhelm and tell him I'm back.'

Nick almost laughed out loud. She didn't get it. They both looked like they'd been in a massacre. 'I'd have a shower first, Tara.'

Tara glanced down at her blood-speckled shorts. Then she looked at him. He was smiling but there were some suspicious marks on him too and she thought again of all he'd seen today.

Pretty horrific for a cocktail waiter. The tears in his eyes when the baby had cried. Lucky guy.

Her mind shifted. And the way he'd dominated the CPR and resuscitated the baby. Her brow puckered and she opened her mouth to ask but they'd reached the gangway.

'Go. I have to get scrubbed and check my staff. We'll meet later.'

Then he was gone and she stared thoughtfully after him. 'Scrubbed?' Odd choice of words. There was more here, she mused in sudden exhaustion as she began to climb the stairs. A passenger looked at her strangely as she passed and she picked up her pace.

Nick was right. So much had happened. She needed a shower. And maybe a long cool drink to think about the last eight hours and the man she'd shared them with.

# CHAPTER SEVEN

WHEN Tara walked into the mess that night there was rumble of chairs being pushed out and everyone stood up and applauded.

She frowned, turned and glanced over her shoulder to see who else had come in but then the captain came across with a huge bouquet of flowers and shook her hand.

'It is for you. This applause. For your amazing skill today and the brilliant outcome.'

It took a moment to sink in. Then all she could think of was that she'd kill Nick for telling and she glanced around until she found him. He was shaking his head.

Something must have shown on her face because the captain chuckled. 'It is not Mr Fender's

fault. I have had the girl's parents on the tele-
phone. They ordered the flowers and send their
gratitude for saving their daughter and grand-
child's lives.'

'Oh. Thank you.' That meant their patient was
still okay. Tara felt relief well inside her and she
smiled. She'd been going to call but had decided
that tomorrow would be a better indication of
the woman's stability. 'So I'm not in trouble for
being back late?'

The captain shook his head solemnly, tongue in
cheek. 'This one time we will forgive you both.'

Her gaze flicked across to Nick, standing beside Wilhelm, and she realised these two were
friends. Wilhelm said something to tease Nick
and Nick punched Wilhelm's arm. Good friends?

A suspicion began to form in her mind and
the events of today and Nick's confident behaviour in the medical crisis meant that suddenly

the crazy idea in her head wasn't a suspicion but blinding truth.

She was about to confirm that with the captain when Nick appeared at her side. 'May I borrow the good doctor, sir?'

The captain waved them away good-naturedly. 'Off you go.'

Tara opened her mouth but before the words tumbled out Nick had steered her to the corner of the room. 'You've guessed my secret?'

He glanced firmly towards the door. Maybe a bit of privacy wouldn't be a bad idea. She didn't know why she was so angry, shattered even, but maybe blurting it out while she was the centre of attention would be a little indiscreet.

Nick read her mind as usual. 'I know you have questions and I'll give my reasons, but please remember I'm not working as a doctor on this cruise.'

She narrowed her eyes at him, nodded and

headed for the door. 'I think I'm too angry to eat right now anyway.'

The breeze off the ocean as she hit the deck was a welcome relief to the heat in her cheeks and she didn't stop at the first rail. Nick caught up and kept pace with her easily as she began to stride towards the bow of the ship.

He glanced down at her. 'I'm sorry.'

She continued to stare straight ahead and walk at a clipping pace. 'That's fine, then.'

He kept beside her. Wondered if she was really trying to walk away from him. 'Never picked you for sarcasm, Tara.'

She stopped. Drilled him with two hard toffee eyes. 'And yet I wondered if you were a liar!'

So she did have a hard streak inside. He guessed she'd have to be or she'd never have survived that long. He liked the idea, though he wasn't sure why, then bit back a smile because if he laughed he'd be really dead. 'Nasty.'

When she looked like taking off again he held up his hand. 'Stop. For a minute. Then you can walk away if you want and I won't follow you.'

She crossed her arms. Not the best listening pose he'd seen but he guessed he deserved it.

Here goes. 'I'm here to substitute for my youngest sister, who fell ill at the last moment. The bar manager gig is her job, a break after med school. And I was a cocktail waiter many moons ago on board the sister ship to this.'

She raised her brows. 'Before med school?'

He sort of nodded. 'Well, after med school. After my parents died I took a break from medicine. I suggested Kiki have one too because I thought she'd lost her cute chuckle. She's got a great one. Usually.'

'What's wrong with your sister?' It was as if she needed to catch him out again.

'Pneumonia.' He hoped she could see there was

no hesitation. 'She hid it until the last, which was why there was such a rush to replace her.'

Another toffee glance. 'Aren't you worried about her?'

'My eldest sister is a respiratory physician. She's with her.'

'Close-knit family. All doctors.' Tara would have loved to have sisters. Or even a brother who cared. One who thought she had a cute chuckle. Or maybe parents who cared. She could feel herself soften towards him and it made her cross again. He had lied to her.

She started to walk on but he could come if he wanted to keep up. 'That doesn't excuse you saying you were good at first aid. Not telling me the truth. I feel like a fool.'

He stopped and she slowed. 'I never intended you to feel that way.' She looked back at him.

'Well, you did.'

'I'm sorry.' He caught up. 'You were in the

zone at the accident, you have more experience than me at crash Caesareans, so I was happy to be back-up and explain later when less important things were going on.'

He crinkled his eyes at her. That was a play. She was sure of it. Shame it worked. 'You said you liked the frivolous cocktail waiter. I didn't think I could stay light and frothy if I was an MD in your eyes.'

There might be just a hint of truth in that. 'So you admit you were dishonest for a reason.'

He raised his brows. 'I got the message you didn't want a constant reminder of what you'd been doing for the last two years.' She couldn't dispute that.

He shrugged but there was a wicked glint in his dark eyes that almost made her smile. 'I was happy to help you relax.'

'Oh. Relax. Is that what we were doing?'

He shrugged and his exposure to Italian charm was obvious. 'Sì.'

'Well, I haven't forgiven you.'

'Early days yet. It's more important you accept my apology.'

She screwed her face up at him. Why was she so cross anyway? Because he was a doctor or because he wasn't a cocktail waiter?

Or was she scared because they did have more in common that she'd planned? Because the man who'd worked beside her today occupied a whole lot more of her thoughts than she was comfortable with, and this trip was about rebuilding her confidence in society, not finding new angst.

'So are you still tired or should we sneak up and grab a couple of deckchairs and check out the movie?'

That sounded so brainless and attractive. She was in no rush to lie on her bed and relive today's events in gory detail, and she had the idea he knew that. See, she shouldn't be second guessing his intentions all the time. Why couldn't she just breeze along and not worry about the what-ifs and subtext? Mentally she folded her arms. She wasn't going to! 'Deckchairs under the stars with checked blankets?'

'One each.' Snapshot of Nick wearing virtue. She couldn't help but smile. He was the guy for amusement all right.

'Do you know what's on?'

'*Titanic*?' He pulled a serious face. 'Could be good practice.'

She so didn't believe him. She was learning. 'Very funny.'

He grinned. 'I think it's a romantic comedy.' He held out his hand suggestively.

She tucked her hand into her side and ignored his offer. She ticked the conditions off on her fingers. 'My own blanket, if you can guarantee no blood, no guts, no death. I'm in.'

The movie hadn't started when they arrived, rows of tucked-up passengers munched on popcorn as they lay back and watched the big screen on the top deck. The ocean sloshed against the hull seventeen floors below, the stars shone above, and rows of lanterns beside the huge screen gave it a carnival feel.

The Casablanca Bar was doing a roaring trade in Irish coffee and hot toddies and after he'd settled her Nick went across and returned with two cappuccinos and a bag of popcorn.

He wanted to feed her again. When he'd put their mugs down on the little tables he nudged his chair closer to hers. He avoided her eyes and wasn't quite whistling innocently.

He could tell Tara was pretending not to notice behind a wall of indifference but he'd bet her mouth ached from trying not to smile.

Insidiously, he could almost see the stress from

the day begin to fade away, even as the introductory credits faded away from the screen.

Nick settled beside her and offered her popcorn from a striped yellow bag he kept hold of. Okay, he was like a big kid, but he wanted her to lean over him. As if he'd said, *Mine.*

She reached and he drew it towards him, she leaned over further and he watched her frown and narrow her eyes at him. She was getting cross.

She sat back. 'Did you have to pay for the popcorn?'

'Nope. It's free.'

'So why didn't you get two?' More glaring and he struggled to keep his smile tucked behind his teeth.

'Because I'm a control freak. Did I tell you that?' The grin escaped. 'Besides, if I got two you wouldn't have to lean over and get some. Think what I would have missed out on.'

'I'll get my own.' She went to stand and he put out his hand to stop her. She avoided his touch because she knew he was laughing. That was a shame. Now he felt bad.

'Seriously, I don't eat popcorn. This is yours.' And he gave it to her with a flourish until she smiled back.

She opened her mouth to say something but he turned to her with a mock admonishing finger. 'Shh. The movie's starting.'

She narrowed her eyes at him and subsided, and he could tell she'd totally forgotten about the stresses of the afternoon.

Tara sighed and had to admit he amused her in an annoying way. Finally she was learning not to take him seriously. Something she'd never practised with Vander. Everything had been serious with him and she wondered why she hadn't seen that before she'd married him.

By the third mouthful of popcorn she'd recovered her good humour and was absorbed in the film.

Tara really enjoyed the movie. Sitting here with Nick was companionable and low key. She didn't have to do anything or be anyone. Just another humped blanket in the dark. Finally. It was amazing how good that felt.

When Nick stopped teasing she really did relax. And there wasn't a drop of blood or hint of violence in the whole ninety minutes, as he'd promised. Or any sinking ships.

Watching a movie with Nick was a hoot. When an unexpected or pivotal moment came, he'd glance across at her as if to check she was enjoying it, she'd glance back and smile. Satisfied mutual enjoyment was there and they'd move on to the next scene.

When she laughed, he'd look across and smile with what looked like real pleasure, and Tara didn't get why he cared but it warmed her that he did. It was the most relaxed she'd ever been, watching a movie with someone. Her parents had thought television an unnecessary evil and she'd been pushed towards reading. In fact, she couldn't really remember the last time she'd watched a movie with someone who was in tune with her like this.

Towards the final scenes Tara knew she didn't want it to end. This whole ambient slice of time. This bubble of fantasy after the horrors of the day. They'd go soon. And Nick would help her up, they'd fold their blankets and she'd trot off to her lonely cabin and lie awake.

Her mood flattened and she wondered why a guy like Nick would want to hang with someone damaged like her anyway.

The hero kissed the heroine and they both shone with the promise of new life together. She could hear the lady next to them sniffing, and someone behind her blew her nose, and Tara just wanted to get out of there before the credits rolled and she had to think again why it was she could never cry. She couldn't even cry when someone was happy, let alone when someone died.

That was never going to happen to her. Too many moments like this and she'd be just setting herself up for a fall. She needed to keep her eye on reality.

Six months recuperating and she'd go back. Take up where she'd left off. A life-saving machine meeting a need someone had to meet.

That's what Vander would have wanted. What she was good at. What her parents would have anticipated for her. She tried to imagine her husband's face but his features were much harder to remember than she expected. She could remember promising she'd keep up his work as he died, though, and she tried not to sigh. Already she knew it was going to be hard to go back.

For some stupid reason she wished she could just explode into noisy sobs.

Enough angst. She faked a yawn and thrust the yellow striped bag at him. 'Sorry, Nick. I'm out of here or I'll fall asleep.' As she looked at him the weariness really caught up with her and she could feel herself droop.

Nick had been thinking of taking Tara's hand for a while now, in fact, but he'd been waiting for the schmoozy part of the film because she could be dangerous to push too quickly. Then they could walk back to her cabin hand in hand and who knew where that might lead?

He'd blown that one well and truly. Not something he could remember doing for a while. He couldn't quite grasp she'd gone before he could even stand up.

Funny how sitting here in the dark, alone, he could remember in vivid detail the feel of her hand in his earlier today. Something simple like that should not have been so memorable, or so desirable.

He watched her walk away, knowing there was no use following, glanced at her empty seat and his hand holding the popcorn.

Unpredictable. Her middle name.

Nick didn't sleep well. He couldn't get the picture of Tara's exhaustion as she'd walked away from him out of his mind. Or the fact that he had been responsible for putting her in the position they'd stumbled on.

He understood why she'd been angry he'd kept his medical background a secret and he'd surprised himself how much it mattered she forgive him for a stupid lie he'd so carelessly started.

Why had he started that? Random bad choice or unadulterated deceit to get into her good graces? Maybe he wasn't such a nice guy after all when he wanted something badly.

The thing was, it was turning out he'd never felt like this before and that came with a whole boatload of concerns. Like he needed to remember that a good time didn't equate with happily-ever-after. Ever.

The weariness in Tara's face should not haunt him and he shouldn't blame himself for making it worse for her. Bringing it all back.

He should have listened to instinct and started with a small morning trip instead of the full day extravaganza he'd planned like the big show-off he was. Then they wouldn't have been anywhere near the scene of the drama.

But then the young mother and her baby would most certainly have died. No way could he wish that.

And there were other things he couldn't wish away.

Memories of Tara's golden eyes gazing raptly from their lunch table at Praiano, her mouth laughing at him from the waves at Positano, and her hand in his as they'd strolled the streets of Amalfi.

Nope, wouldn't give that away either.

It seriously shouldn't have mattered that much if his profession had alienated her.

And why the big rush to show her off to his aunt, or show those places so special to him on the Amalfi coast to Tara? He'd never felt the need to share that with anyone except his sisters, let alone a first date.

What the hell was he thinking? Longer term? Life term? For a woman he'd known a few days who only wanted superficial escape from the horrors of her past? Before she went back?

What if he'd been lying to himself all this time and had been secretly longing to find his deeper soul mate. He laughed out loud and it sounded way too bitter even to him. He'd long ago decided he had no faith in soul mates.

Lord, no. Next he'd be fantasising about baby brunettes and breastfeeding in the family home. That definitely wasn't his style. He wasn't going there and the best way of making sure of that was to steer clear of the whole intense relationship thing like the plague.

To be sensible, today needed to be the first day of avoidance week for him.

So back to happy-clappy flirting in non-specific directions. For safety's sake maybe that should be in directions that pointed anywhere but at the ship's hospital and its junior doctor.

He should listen to his own advice. And just let it all flow. Life was too short to wallow in a might-have-been relationship. Enjoy the view— but don't touch it. Don't touch Tara.

In the corner of his mind a little voice whispered so quietly he barely noticed. The voice wondered what her husband had been like.

The night stretched ahead of him and hopefully

the crew's bar would be extra-busy because he missed her on hour one of avoidance week.

*At Sea*

The next morning Tara decided dodging Nick was a great idea because a fling wasn't a fling when it started to take over your life. When your life started to grow tendrils of excitement with each new facet you discovered of the flingee. That sounded like an obsession.

Or if you couldn't clearly remember your late husband's face.

Of course, avoiding Nick would prove less difficult if the darned man would stop appearing in her dreams. Surely Technicolor reverie was not the only reason she'd woken up with a smile on her face that morning.

The little voice went on to suggest dreams of a tanned and muscular cocktail waiter were immeasurably better than nightmares of the medical dramas and disasters of the last two years, but the jury was out on that idea too.

The cruise only lasted another week and no way was she getting close enough to expose her seeping wounds or open her dark soul for Nick's perusal. Caring involved way too many emotions. She still had such a rock of collected grief and a bitter well of anger from the last two years that it was a wonder she could drag her feet, carrying the weight.

Work. Work would keep her mind where it should be, pleasantly busy, not too close to her patients so she wouldn't get involved, pleasantly distant from her work colleagues so they wouldn't ask about her past or start a discussion about the crash Caesarean at the side of the road that had brought it all back just when she'd been getting some perspective.

For the rest of her time off she would avoid the pool deck and bars. And Nick. That would help.

Tara had a late start today and somehow at breakfast got dragged into auditions by the beauty girls for the final-night crew pageant. She suspected she still looked a fright, though, because one of the girls in the beauty spa she'd treated for a stomach bug/hangover offered a free beauty treatment and under protest Tara now sported new designer eyebrows and a sultry lash tint.

Every time she passed a mirror she couldn't help glancing at the stranger she saw and even though the last thing she wanted to do was appear on stage, even she could see her face was filling out, the lines of strain were easing and there was a new lightness in her step that she hadn't felt for a long time.

It was only a spotlight dance and she could manage that. She'd once been a good dancer but Vander had had no time for frivolous things like dancing or parties.

She was beginning to think that if they'd structured in some down time, maybe the rest of the time in the camp would have been more balanced. Pretty strange that it had taken a cocktail waiter to show her that.

# CHAPTER EIGHT

ONE of Nick's bar staff, George, had burned his hand on the cappuccino machine and even though Nick hadn't started work yet he accompanied him down to the sick bay to assure himself George got there safely. Seemed the responsible thing to do—him being manager.

Nick glanced around the waiting room as they waited, peered behind the desk to see who was in the obs ward and leaned back nonchalantly when Marie arrived to log the new patient.

The door to the consulting room opened and he started to smile but it dimmed a little when Wilhelm appeared to direct the barman into his office. His friend raised his eyebrows at Nick as he hovered, lifted his hand in a sardonic wave, and when Nick continued to stand there he came out.

'She's not here.' Wilhelm shrugged and pretended his ignorance of Tara's whereabouts. 'Not due for another couple of hours.' He lowered his voice.

'You sure she's for you? Don't know if she's your party girl, Nick. Very serious, aloof, you sure you guys are from the same planet? I wouldn't like to see her hurt.'

Since when was Wilhem Tara's new protector? Nick avoided Will's eyes. He'd already seen a side different from serious and aloof. Heck, he'd had her giggling in her seat of the little sports car, before they'd been held up in the traffic.

'She has some issues. But you're right. I don't want to add to them.' He shrugged. 'Just wanted to make sure she's okay after yesterday.'

'Seemed fine when she dropped in for a minute this morning.'

'So she's been in?'

Wilhelm tapped his head as if it all suddenly came back. 'Gone to the crew auditions, I think.'

'Just remembered that, did you?'

'Need to get rid of you so I can do my work.' Wilhelm raised his brows as if to say, *So why are you still here?*

'Thanks.' Nick moved to the door and crossed to the stairway. A sudden excess of energy had him jogging up them two at a time to the next level, where he could cross to the cavernous stage theatre.

They'd been nagging him all week to do a baritone spotlight at the crew pageant and at the time he hadn't been in the mood but the cruise director had hinted about setting an example to his staff and finally he'd agreed. So he had the excuse.

To his delight the first person he saw there was Tara, under her own spotlight on the stage, though less delightful was that she was dancing with Miko, Nick's counterpart on the restaurant side and the suavest man on the ship. They were leaning together to the strains of a sexy salsa.

Tara yelped and the music halted. Miko stepped back off her foot with an apologetic shuffle while Tara rubbed her toes. Even better, as far as Nick was concerned, one of the directors came across and pointed the senior catering officer to the phone. They all knew what that meant.

Nick vaulted over the seats in front of him and disappeared up the side steps into the wings before Tara had a chance to back away. So much for avoidance—it was more like a golden opportunity and he couldn't have stopped his forward momentum if he'd tried.

'I'll take over until Miko comes back,' Nick said nonchalantly as he walked across the stage. The musical director nodded and started the music again.

Nick loved to salsa. He loved it even more with Tara, even if she was still a little stiff in his arms, but she couldn't hide her relief she'd found some-one she could dance with.

'Miko's normally a pretty good dancer,' Nick said, to open the conversation.

She raised her eyebrows and he noticed how her eyes seemed bigger and darker. Something was different.

'I heard that.' She shrugged. 'It's probably me. He's a bit macho.' She mimicked, '"I vill lead this time."' She shrugged. 'I kept getting the steps wrong and I don't like being told what to do. Just couldn't get his rhythm.'

He was happy with that, Nick thought with an internal smile. 'Imagine you not taking orders.' That was supposed to have come out under his breath and Nick glanced again at her face to see if she'd heard.

The brows went up again and he got the

change. New and darker brows. He loved the way women did things like that. No way would he allow someone to reef out his facial hairs for the sake of fashion but she looked even more divine now.

His hands remembered her from when they'd been in the water yesterday as his fingers slid down her arm. Like toffee-coloured silk.

'And whose rhythm am I supposed to get?' she said.

They bumped hips perfectly in time as long as he steered decisively and she agreed to be directed. It seemed she did.

They both knew she fitted into his embrace like a missing link and floated across the stage in unison because she let him lead.

'You tell me.' He spun her away and back again, and she tilted her neck and smiled.

'Nope. Your head will swell again.'

The music came to an end and reluctantly their

hands parted. The musical director came across and grinned at them. 'Guess that's a wrap.' She winked at Nick. 'You want her on stage while you sing to her too?'

Tara's hands still tingled from touching Nick but at that suggestion she looked up. If she wasn't mistaken, Nick even looked a little embarrassed. 'You're singing?' She walked across to the wings. 'I want a good seat for this one.' As far back as possible.

In fact, she needed space because dancing with Nick was like lying in the ocean with him, a journey into sensory overload, every cell aware, recognising, communicating, warning her she'd want more. Like the memory of their skin-to-skin frolic in the Mediterranean, dancing was like being wrapped in a warm buzzing blanket, and she needed to fan her face and get the heck away from him.

So much for avoidance. Tara sincerely hoped

he was a terrible singer. She didn't think she could take any more attraction and any chance for their light and breezy relationship had been further weakened when she didn't have the barrier of their professions to protect her.

No way was she ready to be trapped into a love affair. A lust affair had seemed possible for a woman who had a block of ice where her heart was and just needed it warmed a little.

But being with Nick was having a blowtorch applied to her block of ice and the speed with which she was melting absolutely terrified her. She knew she couldn't risk allowing herself to get close to someone in case they saw how closed she was, or, God forbid, wanted to help her, because if more than the edges of her heart thawed she was at dire risk of drowning in emotion and she didn't know if she'd come out the other side.

With feelings came pain, and regret, then came the kaleidoscope of memories of all those she'd lost and all the guilt and shame and desolation she'd bottled up so long that her tears had withered and died and dried for ever.

If she couldn't be honest and open with herself, no way was she ready to be honest with anyone else—least of all a light-hearted, good-time guy like Nick. No man deserved that.

Nick stepped across to the front of the stage and her turmoil of thoughts froze like a speech bubble in front of her.

Nick began to sing, not loudly without the microphone but somehow the notes drifted to the edges of the huge room in a liquid-chocolate baritone that should be outlawed, especially in a tall black-haired pirate who promised every woman there he would protect and comfort them until the end of the world.

Tara rubbed the goose-bumps that rose on her skin and peripherally she saw others stop, turn, listen, while the women in the audience sort of drifted en masse towards the front of the auditorium.

Tara could feel the flutter of panic as her body responded to the call and she stood shakily and edged her way to the exit. At the last moment she broke into a trot, and as the doors shut behind, her shoulders slumped as if released by a giant hand.

She fought the emotion that clenched like a fist in her chest, something she'd become very good at in the Sudan, and within minutes she had her control back.

No wonder her instinct had told her to run from this man.

Nick saw Tara leave the auditorium and as he finished the song he knew it was no use seeking her out. Even though he'd been singing for her. The applause came out of the dark unexpectedly and he blinked, remembered there were others there, and his mask slipped into place.

'That was amazing, Nick.'

The female director came up and patted his arm. Very friendly woman, this, Nick thought sardonically, and flashed a smile at her.

'I hope you can do a couple of numbers for us. And I think you should be the second last song of the night. Right before the finale with everyone.'

Nick just wanted to get out of here. 'Just the one, Delores. I don't care where it is. I have to get back to work now.'

She touched his arm again and now there was a little group of women hovering and the moment didn't have the usual fillip of amusement he would normally have got out of the attention.

'I'll have to see about that,' she purred, and Nick put his hand in his pocket, ostensibly to retrieve his phone, so her arm fell away.

'Just the one,' he said, and smiled as he glanced at the blank screen. 'Gotta go. Have a good day, everyone.'

A chorus of 'Bye, Nick' floated after him but already his mind was back on Tara.

Waking up the next morning with Santorini above her porthole was like looking at some-one else's travel brochure. She couldn't believe it was real.

Cliff faces soared from the brilliant blue of the Aegean Sea, layered in sedimentary colours from eruption after eruption until you reached the top where the white-painted town sprawled along the ridge and down the sides like white icing dribbling on a cake.

Twenty minutes later, after a visit to the crew's dining room, she still couldn't stop looking. She shook her head and dug her spoon into her break-fast yoghurt. She'd taken to eating at the rail, at the bow of the ship, because it made sure she at least spent some time outside the ship in the sun.

In front of her today were volcanic islands,

pieces left from a once whole volcanic island. She'd never seen so many cruise ships together at once as Santorini was serenaded by the brilliant flotilla of liners anchored off the cliffs.

Snub-nosed tenders ferried passengers from ship to shore, where their gaily garbed passengers could make for the cliff-climbing mules or the cages of the cablecar and the town of Fira.

Tara was rostered on late today, and could have had early shore leave, but she couldn't dredge enthusiasm for shore forays after the last one. The problem was she hated spare time and found it too slow waiting for her shifts to start.

It felt like she spent half her time dressed and watching the clock, waiting for work. No doubt Nick would think she was sick, then she grinned, but Wilhelm seemed to appreciate it.

She leant on the rail but she could sigh at the beauty of the view for a while yet. She drew another deep breath, inhaled the promise of a beautiful day, something she was only just learning again how to do. It felt tentatively good and she vowed one day she'd come back and explore this coastline, and even that tiny step to admitting there was a future out there somewhere lifted her spirits.

She owed Doug for getting her away when he had because she shuddered to think what she'd be like if she'd spent another year buried in disaster. As long as she kept perspective she could thank Nick too for helping her take the first few steps to letting go. She just had to remember he had a twelve-day expiry date.

After half an hour she gave up and headed for the ship's hospital. To heck with waiting, she needed work and maybe there was something she could do before she started her shift.

Maybe she could relieve Will so he could go and do something at the rehearsal. He and Marie had a hoot of a comic act they'd practised.

When she walked in the door she wondered if she'd jinxed herself.

The clinic was overflowing and Tara frowned as she squeezed past two pale-looking young women at the desk. Marie looked up wearily but when she saw who it was her eyes brightened.

'Boy, am I glad to see you. Glad someone caught you. We thought we'd have to page. As you can see, Will's snowed under with this bug that's taken over on level ten. Huge family group and it's spreading like wildfire.'

'Gastro bug? Nasty.' She thought about that in an enclosed space like the ship and winced. 'Have they despatched a cleaning crew to the cabins?'

'The barrier team has gone in to disinfect everything and has isolated the passengers involved.' She looked around the room. 'It all started a couple of hours ago and we have twelve already.'

'Is this a common thing?'

Marie wiped her damp brow. 'No. Thank God. We do drills in case it happens but this is the real thing with a vengeance. The captain wants hourly updates.'

Tara nodded. She had a bad feeling about this. 'I'll find Will and see where he wants me to start.'

Just then the consulting-room door opened and Will showed a passenger out. Tara followed Will into his room when he waved her his way.

Will fanned his face. 'We're in trouble, Tara. This virus is exploding exponentially, and that's the good news.'

Crikey. 'What's the bad news?'

Will slapped his hand over his mouth and threw himself at the handbasin, which he reached just in time before he was ingloriously ill.

When he'd finished Tara handed him a damp

sponge and he mopped his lips. No prizes there. 'I'm guessing that's the bad news?'

There was a knock at the door and Marie stumbled in and shut the door hastily behind her, blocking out the sea of anxious faces in the waiting room. She looked even paler than before. 'I'm sorry I have to go off duty,' she mumbled, and bolted past them into the sluice room, where she was similarly affected to Will.

Will sat wearily on the empty patient's bed and Tara glanced around the room until she tracked the disposable masks. She washed her hands and pulled on a pair of gloves and a mask. Looked at the disposable gowns and pulled one of those on too. 'So I'm going to have to be aware it's incredibly infectious?'

Will sucked in a breath and spoke rapidly through gritted teeth. 'Not something we realised when the first person stumbled in. And it's fast-acting. That was only two hours ago.

And I was careful.' He cast an agonised glance at Tara, shook his head, and followed Marie into the sluice room.

Tara picked up the phone and dialled the bridge. No medals for thinking the captain needed to know this was bad before the hour was up. The captain wanted the names of the nurses off duty and promised her help as soon as he had them tracked. Another disinfecting team would be dispatched and she was to use a different consulting room from the one Wilhelm had been using and seal the area until it could be cleaned.

When he suggested additional medical help she knew what was coming. 'But there are no other doctors on board, are there, sir?'

'Just Mr Fender. I'll send him down.'

Nothing else she could say. 'Thank you, sir.'

The captain summoned Nick to the bridge. 'The hospital is in crisis. I know you intended remaining incognito with your staff but it's too much work for the two nurses and one doctor I have left. Hopefully it's a twelve-hour virus and not a longer one.'

Nick nodded. He'd seen it happen once before on a ship and containment was everything. So much for avoiding Tara. Not his fault, though. There was no way out. His salute was crisp. 'Yes, sir.'

When Nick entered the hospital in his white officer's uniform he couldn't be sorry he'd been called in. Tara looked calm and confident but there was no doubting the relief he saw in her face when she met his eyes.

Tara had segregated the clinic between those with gastrointestinal symptoms and the others. Already exposed, she turned the incidental medical problems, and any liaison with complainers over to Nick.

She pointed to the smallest consulting room

and he nodded and got on with it. That was the last Tara thought for the next few hours as a new wave of sufferers arrived.

Gina, the replacement nurse, began to triage the waiting room until the usual clientele were cleared and then between them they began to make headway in the chaos.

Those mildly affected were sent to their rooms and checked on hourly by the remaining roving nurse, and the more severely affected were sent through to Tara, who medicated, cannulated and pushed intravenous fluids through. As each patient became more stable and were discharged to their cabins, the next would be ushered through and processed.

Tara meticulously washed her hands, changed her masks and gloves and gowns between patients and steadily worked through the list until finally, towards evening, when the loudspeaker announced they were leaving port, the waiting room was nearly empty. The nurse assigned to follow up reported those from earlier in the day were improving and even Wilhelm phoned to say he'd settled to lethargy as opposed to violent spasms.

By ten p.m. it was over. Tara and Nick looked at each other as the last patient was ushered to the door.

Nick shook his head and began to clap slowly. Tara frowned and then accepted her due with as good a grace as she could.

'End of shift,' Nick said.

She was almost too tired to return the favour but dredged up the energy to offer a reluctant smile then inclined her head and put her hands together and slow-clapped him back.

The nurses peered out to see what was happening and Nick and Tara applauded them too. They all smiled at the empty room and groaned collectively. That made them all smile again, wearily.

'Bags first shower,' Tara said with a feeble attempt at a joke, and there was a chorus of agreement. 'You were all amazing. What a team. Thank you so much.'

'I'll finish tidying up here,' Nick said. 'You ladies deserve to go.' The nurses grinned and bolted before he could change his mind.

'I'll stay too.' Tara couldn't leave him to do that. She was the medical officer in charge.

'I'll do it, Tara. Go.'

There he was again. That bossy person she'd glimpsed before. And she hated taking orders. But it did sound temptingly attractive. To hell with being territorial, she felt like a wreck. A possibly infectious wreck. He could win this one, bugs and all. 'Fine. Thanks.'

Nick waved her away with a suspiciously straight face and it seemed a long way up the three flights of stairs to her cabin because her legs reminded her she'd been on them non-stop for twelve hours.

Ten minutes later the steamy water was cascading over her scalp and face and she sighed as she leant her forehead against the shower wall. The wall was solid. Like Nick.

In fact, he was a bit of hero, staying back so she could be here.

The water ran down her shoulders and between her breasts and the heat soaked in, and as she lathered with her favourite violet soap, the tension from the day seeped away down the plughole with the suds.

Nick sure was a hero with his unfailing good humour today under trying circumstances. Some of the passengers had been very unhappy and determined to blame the ship's food. Nick had very gently but clearly explained that apart from one family and friends no others were sick, which meant one of their members had brought the virus on board and spread it between them.

Yep, a hero. Her mind drifted back to that dance in the auditorium—where she'd somehow forgotten those fifty eyes watching them—and how she'd spun in his arms and in sync like no other dance she'd ever had, and she still blushed at the thought.

Then his song in the dark, his deep, dark voice steeling around her heart with velvet fingers until she'd had to flee. The guy had some serious mojo going on there.

Even after the twelve exhausting hours of exposure today, his infallible good humour and caring expertise all made her feel good. And that was what she was looking for.

Right? Just to start feeling good for a change.

So meeting Nick had been a good thing. He made her forget the horror of the last two years.

Made her smile. Made her want him to smile.

Glimpses she'd caught of him ushering in the next patient, his compassionate dealings with the children and the way he'd lifted spirits when the nurses had become stressed, and even the occasional wink he'd sent her way as they'd passed in the waiting room had made her giggle.

Crazily, she thought with a sigh, even the back of his neck as he'd passed her by left a good feeling in the pit of her stomach.

The shower spray cascaded over her and she sighed with the bliss of it. She was *not* going to think about his backside because she'd very recently discovered a previously unknown fetish for slim male hips and taut backsides. It seems they turned her on. When had she become a voyeur?

She lifted her head and let the water run over her face as if she could wash away the growing awareness of everything about Nick Fender that persisted despite her feeble attempts at denial.

Very feeble because that reaction to thinking about Nick twirled a baton in her belly like that of a drum majorette and she shifted her feet on the tiles as if she could step away from it.

'Get out of my head.' The words echoed in the bathroom and she ducked her face out of the stream. So now she was going barking mad. And her legs even wobbled as her knees seemed to soften when pictures of Nick sashayed into her mind. Now, bizarrely, her stomach had started to tremble with the fantasy sensation of Nick rubbing the tension from her shoulders like he had that day in the ocean.

Her breasts were suddenly too receptive to the rush of sensation, too responsive to the heat, too reactive to the thought of Nick's long fingers rolling her suddenly aching tips.

She snapped the shower onto cold, then off, and grabbed for a towel. Her face felt as red as the floral arrangement in the bowl on the table.

The distant sound of the doorbell penetrated from the room beyond.

She tilted her head and heard it again. How long had that been ringing? Tara wrapped her hair in the towel and grabbed the white robe from the back of the door, and as she crossed the room she could see the missed-call light on the phone beside the bed.

She quickened her step. Hoped it wasn't a dire medical emergency. At this time of the night it could be little else.

Nick stepped back as Tara opened the door and his breath hissed out with relief that she looked fine. More than fine, really, with her honey-gold neck exposed like a swan and a towel holding her hair high on her forehead.

Damned if she wasn't naked under the robe. And wet. His gaze skimmed down to the trickles of water running down her legs. A diffusing trail of soapy steam stretched out behind her, laden with the elusive scent of violets, and he tried not to lean towards her to inhale.

His gut kicked and he couldn't regret what had obviously been a dumb impulse. He'd tried to ring her after his shower and let her know he'd do the early shift in the hospital so she could come in later.

When she hadn't answered he'd got it into his brain she'd come down with the bug and was lying miserably ill alone in her room.

He lifted his gaze to her face because that was a lot safer than imagining what was on display under the white robe she was hastily tying. 'So you're okay!' he said.

He loved the way her forehead puckered when she frowned. 'Yes, I'm okay. Why wouldn't I be?'

He was a fool. Now a turned-on fool. And he'd disturbed her when she needed her rest more than anyone. He needed his fantasies back in their box.

'Sorry I bothered you. Maggot in the head.' He turned away, cursing himself so hard he almost missed her soft reply.

'Nick?'

He jerked to a stop as if she'd pulled a string taped to his back. Turned to see a whimsical little smile that lifted his spirits miraculously as she leaned towards him with her foot in the doorway to stop the door shutting her out in the hallway with him. 'Can you come here for a sec? Please?'

He finished the turn and took a couple of steps until he was right beside her, could smell her skin again, and then, to his delight, she leant up and kissed him on his cheek. A feather-light brush of lips that reverberated through his psyche way out of proportion to the pressure.

'Thanks for today. You were wonderful,' she said softly.

The last thing he'd expected. She'd been the amazing one. He jammed his hands into his pockets to stop himself pulling her into his arms and kissing her thoroughly and then some, then blurted out the first thing that came into his head. 'I didn't see you flagging.'

'I would have if I'd had to manage on my own.' She pushed herself back against the doorframe. 'Anyway, see you tomorrow.'

Tomorrow. He breathed. Pulled his hands from his pockets and pushed then down the outside of his legs. Relaxed his fingers and kept them there. 'That's what I came to say. The captain's rostered me in the hospital another day. I'll do the early clinic and you can come later. Sleep in.'

She nodded. 'I'll be back after breakfast.'

'Make it lunch. I'm good for it.' His words hung in the air and he wondered how something so innocent could create such double meaning.

'I'll see if I sleep.' More hidden meanings? He wished.

'Stay in bed anyway.' Banished that thought from his brain. White sheets, Tara's hair spilled across the pillow, honey skin bare and silken soft under his hands.

She opened her mouth to argue but he was ready for her if she did. Maybe she knew that because all she said was, 'Then you'd better go to bed.'

That was when the devil stepped in. Made short work of the restraints he'd placed on himself, pushed him in the back so that he was propelled into saying it out loud. 'Don't suppose you'd like to invite me in?'

He couldn't banish the vision of him walking in and closing the door with both of them inside. To stand behind that door and feel the length of her against him, backing slowly towards the bed they both wanted.

Tara saw Nick's eyes darken. This was her fault. The kiss! As soon as she'd done it Tara had known she shouldn't have kissed him. Well, it had rocked her just as much. Even that feather-light caress across his raspy cheek had made her knees weaken and turn to jelly, like she was standing back in the shower. Naked. Wet. Imagining him.

Now she really could taste him. Inhale that aftershave that she'd forever associate with Nick. She passed her tongue over her lips and drank in the sight of the real thing. Here he was. Fantasy Nick.

Her new favourite scent. When had that happened? Her body still thrummed with wicked fantasies that surely you were allowed in the privacy of your own shower stall, for goodness' sake. How was she to know he was going to turn up at her door, his hair still damp from his own shower, the half-open shirt exposing his strong chest and throat so that she wanted to bury her nose in him.

Her suddenly rapt gaze hovered over that throat. She saw him swallow and she followed the movement. Drifted down over his abs, taut against the material of his shirt, his black jeans snug on his slim hips, the unmistakable tightness across the front tweaking the centre of her with just the thought.

She'd been quietly excited about what she would share with Vander after their marriage, but sex had been such a small part of their relationship she'd tried not to be disappointed. All she knew was she'd never wanted a man like she wanted this one right here, right now.

Please.

If she asked him, he'd stay. She was sure of it. Did she want that? She should feel ashamed, thinking that. A one night stand screamed shipboard romance and loose woman. But suddenly the idea of walking away after a week with flesh-and-bone memories seemed infinitely better then walking away with a hollow fantasy.

She dragged her eyes away, drawn back to his face, his mouth. The air crackled with awareness, attraction imploding into need.

She licked her lips again. Her head was talking so much she couldn't remember what had been said out loud. 'Did you say something?'

'I said, do you want to invite me in?'

Then she said, 'Lord, yes.' His eyes flared. 'But I don't think so.'

He blinked. Not surprised but definitely disappointed. 'Very sensible.'

She smiled but she could feel the vulnerability in it. The fine line between changing her mind or being safe. If he'd pushed it would have been easier to say no but he was ever the gentleman. 'Goodnight, Nick.'

A final glint of mischief. 'It could be.'

They stared at each other and Tara wondered what was stopping her from just reaching out and touching his hand. That was all it would take. One movement on her part. She was a grown woman. A widow, not some teenage girl who needed the illusion of love to bestow her gift.

Maybe this was the way to healing. To finding her path back to the woman she'd been before the Sudan, maybe before she'd tried so hard to be everything Vander had thought she was. Before she'd failed.

Nick didn't have expectations of perfection. He couldn't have because she'd arrived here a wreck and he'd still befriended her.

Maybe if she kissed him again, just once more, properly, she'd know what she really wanted to do.

# CHAPTER NINE

NICK had accepted the no. Expected it. That wasn't to say he didn't carry condoms in his wallet.

So when he saw Tara's pupils dilate he was willing to adapt. Even so, when she leant towards him one more time, he hadn't intended the kiss to get quite so carried away. But he'd wanted this with a depth of need he hadn't anticipated.

The devil whispered.

They both wanted this. Both grown adults.

Suddenly they were plastered together and before he knew it they were through her door and across the room and up against a wall in her cabin, lost to the rest of the world.

One hand captured her head and he couldn't

get enough of her delectable mouth, while the fingers of his other slipped inside her robe and captured the silken, peaked glory of Tara in his palm.

Her indrawn shudder softened his mouth and he raised his face and breathed in her hair before his lips skidded down the side of her cheek, skin so soft, so vulnerable, like the petals of a blushing rose, until he found her mouth again.

'I could kiss you for ever.'

'Nick.' A whisper back against his lips.

'Hmm?' He opened his eyes and eased away so that she wasn't jammed against the wall. Ran his hands down her back in apology. Gazed down at the open robe and the perfection that was Tara and lost the plot again. Leaned in.

'Nick.' Another whisper.

He shook himself. 'Sorry. Yes?'

She was smiling. And what a smile, but the

vulnerability had grown. He felt his insides melt and rush of emotion he didn't recognise.

'I'm not very good at this. Never have been.'

Nick shook his head. She was incredible. He pulled her even closer and hugged her. 'It takes two to tango. And you are perfect.'

'Not what my husband said.'

He held her soft bony bits against him. 'Then he was a fool…' and a creep, Nick thought but didn't say it '…who didn't know how lucky he was.'

But he saw her fear of letting him down, saw the undermining of her self-belief, her lack of faith in her natural instincts, and for the first time he decided cholera wasn't all bad if it had carried off Tara's husband.

'So why did you marry him?' Stupid time to ask this but suddenly he had to know. Not something he'd ever cared about with other women in his arms. Especially a semi-naked one.

'He was a friend of my parents. From their church. And I'd just been let down by a man I thought I'd loved. Who turned out to be married.' She shrugged. 'I thought at least I'd get no lies from Vander.' She sighed. 'Could have done with a few less home truths.'

'Hey.' Nick tilted her chin. 'Maybe he did lie. About the part of you that scared him.'

He kissed her and when she responded, when she'd relaxed again from the tension he'd created by asking, he slid one finger under her chin until she looked at him again.

'Crazy woman. Can't you see the seductress inside you? She's one hot lady. The one who captured my attention from the first moment I saw you.'

She looked away. Shook her head. 'I was a wreck.'

'Not to me.' He kissed her and when she opened her eyes again he stared straight into them. 'You are the most beautiful and sexy woman I have ever seen.'

She lowered her eyes. Unconvinced. 'Can we go to bed?'

Yes, please. And he would prove it to her. He bent, slid his hands behind her shoulders and knees and lifted her until she was safe in his arms. Squeezed her to him and the robe fell open further. Gentle hills and valleys stretched out before him, silver pale in the dim light, and the darker toffee from her exposure to the sun like a chocolate frame around the white centre of her sweetness. The pink in her cheeks deepened at the way he cherished her with his eyes and he had to kiss her again before he moved. 'Quite happy to stay here and just look—but your wish is my command.'

He carried her gently to the bed, settled her like the feather she was onto the white bedspread, and gazed down at her unwrapped like a morsel at Christmas. 'You are an incredibly beautiful woman.'

When he said it again, for the first time she almost believed him. Her mother had always said she was plain. Vander had once said she was pretty but she didn't want to think about him now. The way Nick was looking at her at this moment was a gift greater than she'd expected and she pulled him down towards her and kissed him. She could take this moment and cherish it. The last two years had taught her a lot and life could disappear at a whim. No way was she going to regret time she shared with Nick.

Nick was in no hurry. 'I'd like to savour this time with you.' He trailed his finger down her cheek, leaned in and kissed her gently but thoroughly, and like magic she relaxed bonelessly back onto the bed under him and he followed her. Forgot what he was going to do as he was lost in Tara, couldn't stop these long, slow, drugging kisses that he'd never really included in his repertoire until today. Kisses that came from a well of need he hadn't known he had. A need that was matched by Tara's because when he went to move she pulled him back and they both drifted away again.

He murmured against her lips, 'You are the most glorious kisser.'

Tara opened her eyes. Her brain screamed, *Not true*, but the sexy curve of his mouth said she had to believe him. She felt the tears scratch, but not form, as a piece of her heart broke off that this gorgeous man thought she was a good kisser.

She of the B minus in the bedroom.

And she had to believe him because he was looking at her as if she was the eighth wonder of the world. Nobody had ever looked at her like that before.

So she pulled him back and opened her soul for some more of the same and slowly his hands began to worship her. And he encouraged her gently to do the same to him.

When he moaned, she stopped until he encouraged her on and slowly she began to smile. Began to seek those movements that tortured him, nibbled at the edges of knowledge that was growing, nibbled at the edges of Nick with a curve of her lips that made Nick smile back, and they murmured on through the night. Learning, teasing, sometimes devouring, and occasionally dozing.

Much later Tara rested back in Nick's arms and traced the taut curve of biceps. 'Oh, my. So that's what they mean by sexy and satisfied.'

Nick smiled and squeezed her shoulders. He felt ten feet tall and he never wanted to let her go. So why did it feel like his heart was going to break?

Because he didn't do this stuff. The lying back and loving. It was supposed to be all light and fluffy and giggly…and then he was gone.

He leaned across and kissed her forehead. She'd be gone in a week. And he'd be gone in the other direction. This was dangerous territory and he'd survived this long because he knew the rules. Get out. Now.

But he had to kiss her one more time, which led to more, and afterwards he just closed his eyes for a moment. Soon he'd get up and go.

An hour before dawn he left. 'You are amazing.' He shifted his arm out from under her and tried not to see the way her face stilled when she realised he was going. The ridiculous thing was he didn't want to go. Ached to lie the whole full night just listening to her breathe, or moan, but if he didn't get out now something bad was going to happen. He just knew it.

Nick left and Tara lay in her tumbled bedclothes and sighed at the ceiling with a soft incredulous smile on her face. Her arms crept around her tender breasts and she just had to hug herself. Her body still glowed in a languidly sated way. There was so much to learn and Nick cared enough to show her a world she had never known existed.

She shied away from the reminder that this world had six nights to go and even with the way she'd opened to Nick last night she knew there was a closed-off centre he'd never reach. But she felt way more alive than yesterday. 'Oh, my.'

Nick didn't go to bed. He walked the pre-dawn decks like an automaton, head up, peripherally avoiding obstacles and late-night revellers, but only seeing Tara as he'd left her. It had just been sex. But she'd gazed up at him like he was some kind of god, when in fact he was the other bloke. The one with the horns.

The gift she'd given him was priceless. Her faith in him, her belief that he could be trusted with teaching her about her own innate sensuality, allowing him to see into her damaged core of self-belief when it hurt her to show anyone.

The responsibility for that sat like the weight of the whole ship was on his shoulders. What if he let her down? Which he would when he left.

She'd better not fall for him because he felt guilty enough. He was no hero and she deserved one. A genuine one.

If Tara wanted fun and fluff, that's what he was offering. Just sex.

As a middle child and the only boy in the family, he'd always tried to be the opposite of his serious sisters.

He'd had to cut himself off from all the girly stuff like crying and analysing emotions to protect his masculinity and the belief that he was solely responsible for his own happiness. With his mother's betrayal exposed, he couldn't be the rock, 'cos even though he loved women he didn't trust love. He'd lost that trust on the same day.

He didn't want to get too close or be depended on by any woman. Because he knew he couldn't depend on them and they couldn't depend on him.

Except maybe for Kiki. His youngest sis. The one he was replacing now. She'd been all for taking the fun side of life and he'd encouraged her. She had no issues that he was the playboy and entertainer of the family. That was his job.

Had he been stuck in a groove? Did he really want more? No! And if it was changing then he'd put a stop to it right now.

They were docked at Piraeus, for Athens, when Tara turned up at the hospital at ten the next morning. Nick was showing a worried young mum and her baby into his room. Good.

That gave her a minute to let her blushes die down before she had to face him because, to her surprise, after he'd left she'd actually slept the sleep of the very wicked!

She didn't know about dreamlessly because when she'd woken up she'd had a grin plastered on her face like the Joker out of *Batman*. She suspected the dreams had been almost as amazing as the real thing.

Tara followed him into the examination room when he smiled and inclined his head and there was just a flash of naughtiness that made her compress her lips and look at the floor.

When she looked up at the patient she noticed the child's eyes had that exhausted, rolling back look that sick infants had. Her gaze sharpened. Last night receded even further as she studied the infant.

Nick's voice rumbled quietly as she visually assessed the patient. 'I'm Dr Fender, Nick, and this is Dr McWilliams, my colleague. She's very experienced with children.'

Tara smiled. 'Hello.'

The mum gave a perfunctory smile and then

looked worriedly down at her baby. 'Joey's eight months old. He's got a cough and he's crying a lot.'

Nick leaned forward and gave Joey the end of his tie to hold. Tara loved the way he did that while he used his stethoscope to listen to Joey's chest. Then he ran his fingers gently over Joe's skull and even though Tara knew he was checking Joey's fontanelle wasn't sunken, the sight made her stomach warm. He was so gentle and caring that even a baby recognised he was safe with him. Even *she* felt safe with him.

When he'd finished Nick prised Joey's fingers free and stepped back to reach for the thermometer, which he slid under Joey's arm. Joey wriggled and whimpered and Nick gave him back the end of his tie. 'I can hear some rattles in Joey's chest.' The thermometer beeped and Nick pulled it out. He looked at the mum. 'Thirty-nine degrees Celsius. Or a hundred and two point two in Fahrenheit. So he has a temperature. When did you first think he was unwell?'

Aimee's concern deepened. 'Last night. He wasn't feeding as long as he usually does and he felt hot.'

Joey started to cough and Nick and Tara looked at each other with mutual concern. Joey's lips were tinged blue and Tara crossed the room and came back with the little pulse oximeter, which she clipped onto Joey's wrist, and a mask connected to oxygen, which she held off using until they had a reading in room air.

Nick put his hand gently onto Joey's to keep his hand still, and finally they could read the result. Joey's oxygen saturation was down at ninety per cent instead of around a hundred.

Tara waved the mask. 'He needs a little bit more oxygen than he can get out of the air, so do you mind if we pop a little mask on him?'

Aimee nodded tearfully as Tara slipped the

oxygen onto Joey's face. It was a measure of how unwell he was that the little boy didn't fight her.

Aimee wrapped her arms around her own chest. 'I should have brought him earlier.'

'Children go down quickly. You did the right thing.' Tara had wanted to say that but Nick beat her to it and she loved him for it.

Vander would never have said it, even though Aimee was here and had done the right thing.

Nick went on. 'Joey's picked up a chest infection, and I'm afraid he needs to be admitted to the hospital.'

Aimee looked at Tara. 'Can't you keep him here?'

Tara shook her head. 'I'm sorry. No. We could if we had to, if we were out at sea. But, like Nick said, children go down very quickly and we're in a major port. It's safer for Joey to be under the care of a paediatrician in Athens in a proper hospital. He needs intravenous antibiotics, nebulisers to help break up the gunk in his chest and follow-up X-rays.'

Aimee chewed her lip. 'But I can't speak Italian.'

Tara nodded sympathetically. 'That's going to be hard.' She'd found it difficult enough the other day even though the senior staff she'd dealt with had all been able to speak English. 'But your specialist will probably speak much better English than your Italian.'

Nick glanced at his watch. 'Tara's come to take over from me here. You'll need an escort anyway and I've got time to take you. I speak fluent Italian. We'll get an ambulance because Joey needs oxygen.' He squeezed Aimee's arm. 'How about that?'

He met Tara's eyes over the top of Aimee's head and she nodded. He wondered if he would normally have got involved like this. Pre-Tara. He could feel the changes, the idea of taking his care a little further with his patients. Like she did. Nick closed off that train of thought.

He went on, 'I'll get you settled before I leave you. Find an interpreter you're comfortable with.'

They were lucky Nick was here, Tara thought, and she couldn't help being proud of the care he was giving. He was a great guy.

It seemed Aimee thought so too. 'Would you? Thank you.'

Tara listened with half an ear as she settled Joey into a cot and checked his oxygen was attached properly. She wrote down the readings of both oxygen and oximeter and took Joey's pulse.

Nick touched her shoulder and she looked up. 'I'll start the arrangements and see what antibiotic the hospital wants us to start him on. We can give his first dose before he goes.'

Nick realised he was finding it hard to work with Tara. Harder than before. Not to the detriment of his work but to reassure himself that she was still there. Still felt the same. Wasn't regretting last night. Stuff he didn't need on his mind.

She was looking at him like he was a hero again. 'I'll put a cannula in, then,' she said, 'so we can give the antibiotics IV?'

She'd be better at it than him. So whose fault was that? He handed children onto a paediatrician, whereas Tara had had no choice but to gain the skills.

'Thanks. That would be great. I'll send Gina in to help while I phone around.'

Nick and Aimee left with Joey in the ambulance an hour later. Gina tidied up and restocked while Tara finished off the computer notes before she emailed them, together with all the observation and medication charts they'd used, on to the hospital.

The clinic was finished and Tara locked up as she left. She had two hours until she was needed back at work and the idea of a lunchtime nap in her cabin was more attractive than food. Funny how a night making love made you tired.

# CHAPTER TEN

TARA fell asleep with a smile on her face as soon as her head touched the pillow and woke an hour and a half later with the afternoon sun streaming in the window. She stretched, ached a little in odd places and her mouth curved, but she felt fantastic.

The phone rang and she picked it up still half-asleep.

'Have you had lunch?'

'Hello, Nick.' I was just thinking about you. Tara smiled into the phone. 'No. But probably won't have time. I have to be at work in twenty minutes.'

'I'm on my way.' The phone went dead.

She looked at the silent receiver, shrugged and

put it down. Then she assimilated his statement and bounced off the bed and into her bathroom, where she cleaned her teeth and brushed her hair just in time.

The doorbell buzzed.

Her stomach rumbled and when she opened the door Nick was holding a covered plate on a tray.

'You're trying to fatten me up.'

Nick winked. 'Lucky you.'

Tara took the tray and went back to put it on her table, and Nick followed. 'Chicken salad rolled in a wrap. I saw you have one the other day.'

'Quick and easy to eat and just what I fancied.' She glanced at him. 'When did you see me eat?'

'The day before Amalfi. I watched you come in but you didn't see me.'

'And you didn't say hello.'

'I was scoping you out.'

Tara chewed the bite she'd taken thoughtfully.

'Why are you always feeding me?' He didn't answer.

'Don't get me wrong. It's nice.' She pointed to the tiny dish of hulled strawberries that had appeared every day, fresh on her table, since the first day he'd sent them.

Nick looked away. 'You like strawberries. They're good for you.'

She frowned. 'Yes, but *why* are you feeding me?'

She realised he was actually feeling uncomfortable. The moment stretched and Tara wished she hadn't asked.

Nick's problem was that he didn't know why. It just made him feel good. But that was a dumb thing to say. And he couldn't say it was because she was too skinny when, in fact, to him she was perfect.

A new fetish? He'd never wanted to feed a woman before. Though he could remember when Kiki had been sick as a child he'd ride to the shops on his pushbike and bring her home sweets.

The devil helped him out. 'Maybe I like to watch your mouth and it gives me an excuse.'

He watched her blush and lick her lips nervously, and he realised it was true. He really liked watching her mouth. 'But you have to get to work and this conversation could lead to you being late.' He stood up. 'And I know how you hate to be late.'

Tara fought down the heat in her cheeks and concentrated on normal things. Served her right for asking such a stupid question. She realised he had changed out of his whites and was back in the black trousers of the hospitality staff. 'So you're going back to being a bar manager now.'

'Just this afternoon. Though if you get snowed under the captain will probably let me come back for an hour or two. I'll still do the early shift tomorrow, you do the mid-morning and Will should come back in the afternoon.'

So she wouldn't get to see him at work any more today. Funny how after two days she was used to working with him. Would miss his smile. 'So when will we catch up?' Even to her own ears she sounded needy and she wished the words back in her mouth.

They'd both said they were there for the fun and not the future. Nick had also said, 'Never say never,' but that was a just a line from a smooth guy and they both knew that.

Thankfully his response let her know he was still fine with a bit of clinging. 'We could share dinner. I could watch your mouth again.'

He made her smile so easily. It was going to be hell when this cruise ended. 'Same time. Same place?'

'Sounds good.' He turned back at the door and

stepped up to her. Dropped a kiss on her lips that
had her eyes shut one second into it.

When he lifted his head they were both a little spaced. 'Mmm. Like to do more than look
sometimes.'

Then he was gone and Tara was late.

Dinner was a blur because the whole time Tara
was waiting for the time they could finish and
go. She had no idea what she ate. And judging
by the darkness of Nick's eyes, his mind wasn't
on nutrition either.

He held her hand all the way back to her cabin
and she didn't remember much of that trip either. She fumbled the swipe of her card in the
door, tried again without success, and Nick took
it from her and did the deed himself. Then he
stepped back to allow her to enter and followed
so close behind she could feel the heat from
his body.

She stopped suddenly so that he bumped into her and she was grinning when she turned. 'Excuse me?'

'Certainly.' Then not much more was said as their clothes seemed to peel away along with the conversation and Nick lifted her so that her legs were wrapped around him and she was hard up against solid muscle.

Looking down was amazing. His face so chiselled and alive, clearly wanting her, his body sculpted and powerful, holding her as if she weighed little more than a feather, her skin plastered to his as he backed up towards the wall.

His thigh nudged against hers. 'Have you any problems with this wall tonight, my love?'

My love? She wished but she wasn't going there. She grabbed hold of the cold that seeped in with her own acknowledgement of illusion and forced it away. Tonight she was his love. That's all she wanted. She dug her fingers into the rippled muscles of his shoulders and bent down to gently bite his neck. 'I love this wall tonight.'

He growled softly in his throat and she felt the beast within herself respond and not much more was thought, all was sensation, and want, and need, and Nick. And the wall.

Afterwards, as they lay entwined back on her bed where Nick had carried her, chest heaving, silly grins on their faces, Nick stroked a line between her breasts. 'Kissing's not all you're amazing at.'

'I've had a good teacher.' She stroked his chest in turn. 'And you are amazing. Wanna play again?'

He shifted his arm. 'I've got the late shift.' The second lie he'd told her. But inside he was still shaking.

This had been too much. Too amazing. Transcending 'just sex' and lust and all the other names for the things people did when they were searching for this moment he'd shared with Tara.

The moment he hadn't been searching for.

When the earth had spun off its axis like it wasn't supposed to.

'I have to go.'

She frowned. 'You didn't say that earlier. At dinner?'

He didn't meet her eyes. 'I had other things on my mind.' He kissed her and rolled off the bed. Glanced back over his shoulder at her. 'I was watching your mouth.'

To his relief she closed her eyes and giggled. Though that hurt even more. He turned his back and picked up his shirt from the floor. Scooped up the rest of his clothes and disappeared into her bathroom.

Stared at himself in the mirror when the door was shut and hated the man looking back at him with a passion born of fear. He was falling in love with her and he didn't want to.

Another amazing night's sleep and Tara bounced out of bed in the morning, scooped up her yoghurt from the mess, and ate it as she walked towards the hospital.

When she arrived, Nick was showing out Gwen and Tommy, and Tara waved at them. Gwen looked happy, which was nice for a change, and Tara vaguely wondered what the problem had been this time.

'Satisfied customer,' Tara murmured as she followed Nick into the consulting room. She wasn't sure if she was talking about the patient's mother or herself. That made her ears heat.

This man could charm the birds off the trees, let alone cheer up a harassed mother on a ship. And now she came to think about it, she'd seen Gwen yesterday and the day before that as well.

Gwen did seem a tad over-protective. The boy had his arm in sling and the woman smiled at Nick as she left, like he'd made her day.

She looked again. 'What's with Gwen? And Tommy? Boy, is she having a holiday with problems.'

'Sorry?' When he turned back to Tara Nick wasn't smiling, although she thought his eyes did soften when he looked at her. Maybe his gaze did drift over her face as if he needed to see something good.

And he thought that was her? Was she becoming needy?

She resisted the urge to lean up and kiss him.

Nick had gone back to frowning. 'What do you mean?'

Thank goodness she hadn't moved on the kiss impulse. 'Um. Gwen. With Tommy. She's been in most days, I think?' Because now she could see he was on a totally different planet from her at this moment.

She tried not to be disappointed. 'I think Tommy and cruising don't mix.'

Nick clicked on the computer and scrolled back through the doctor's notes. 'Every day, in fact.'

He was looking past her. She thought he'd forgotten she was there until he began to speak in a cold, distant voice she'd never heard him use before. 'A long time ago, when I first started private practice, I met a woman who scared the hell out of me. Gwen reminds me of her.'

'What do you mean?'

'That woman was the wife of a friend. And I tried not to see what was happening. But I became more suspicious every time she came with her little girl. A beautiful little girl I let down.'

Tara didn't like the sound of that. So much so she wished he'd stop, but perversely she needed to hear it as much as he needed to tell the story.

'In the end she nearly killed that little girl and I almost let it happen. I went off and did a stint on a cruise ship while she continued to make that child suffer. You can't always believe what you want to, Tara.'

He looked at Tara and frowned. 'I may have a nasty, suspicious mind but I'd like to rule out something more serious before that mother does any more damage.'

Tara blinked. She turned back to look at the empty waiting room. The woman had gone. 'You think she's making the child's illness up?'

He tapped the computer screen and the list of visits. 'Have a look at how many times she's come to the clinic. We've had one presentation every day since we sailed. All different reasons. All gaining her lots of sympathy for having a sick child.'

He ran his hand through his hair. 'Today was a red rash on the arm that had suddenly appeared.'

He chewed his lip. 'She's given me a list of allergies a mile long, some different from what she's given Wilhelm.'

'So?' Tara couldn't see where this was going. 'She's over-protective?'

He sighed and ran his hand through his hair before he went on.

'She seemed pretty excited about how painful it looked and that set my alarm bells off. I remember that and I'll never forget it.' He glanced at Tara. 'This may seem incredibly far-fetched, but have you ever heard of Munchausen syndrome?'

Tara's brain clicked back into medical mode—away from memories of last night. 'Like a hospital addiction syndrome? They make up illnesses to gain attention? Even have surgery for fictitious illnesses?'

Tara had trouble imagining that in the context of her last two years and survival being paramount to her patients instead of gaining attention.

He nodded. 'And then there's Munchausens by proxy, which is even worse.'

Tara took a step back in shock. 'You mean she could be harming her child to gain attention.' She shook her head vehemently. 'Surely not. I've never seen a case.'

Tara could feel Nick's agitation and she tried to remember what Wilhelm had said after the mother had left the day before.

'I have. Not pretty.' Nick was still in the past. 'That mother's child nearly died before the state removed her. I came back. Saw the damage. Diagnosed my patient with psychosis and she's still in an institution. Her husband, my friend, almost killed himself with remorse. And I had suspicions before I went away. I was one of many who ignored the signals. Because I was having such a good time playing locum, I almost didn't come back and make the diagnosis.'

He rolled his shoulders as if the weight of those memories sat heavily on him, and in a moment of clarity she saw that frivolous Nick had his own nightmares, like she did.

In his normal voice Nick said, 'I just wonder if our Gwen has rubbed something irritating onto Tommy's skin to make it red.'

Tara winced and her stomach tightened with distress. She visualised the pale child who'd just left. 'That's ghastly. Tommy's only just turned three.' She shook her head. They had horrors out here in the real world too.

'Surely not.' She worried her lip with her teeth. What if it was true? 'What were you thinking? What can you do?' What could they do?

Nick lifted his head and there was no lightness in his sea-blue eyes. Today they were cold, reflecting the steel in his voice, and she felt the chill go right through her. She hoped he never looked at her like that.

'We can try and catch her out.' She could see him clenching and unclenching his fingers and she wanted to soothe him from whatever guilt was eating him up.

'Okay.' She touched his hand and his fingers stilled as he looked at her. 'How, Nick?'

He shifted his hand out from under hers and jammed it through his hair. 'I've asked her to bring him back in half an hour to see if the cream works. I've given her lots of sympathy so she should be feeling good and maybe craving a little more attention.' There was a thread of self-disgust in his voice she didn't think he deserved.

'You didn't know.' He wasn't listening.

'Then if I knocked on her door in fifteen minutes? See if I can catch her in the act of trying to make the rash look worse before she comes down here?'

This was no light and airy cocktail waiter. This was a man willing to stick his neck out for a child who might be at risk. Tara tried to visualise the scene. 'Can you do that?'

Action Nick was a whole different person and she was having trouble merging the two Nicks. She didn't know if she'd be so decisive about a suspicion but then she doubted she would have even suspected a mother of such a thing. She was more used to mums worrying about finding enough food for their children than manufacturing illnesses.

Nick glanced at his watch. 'I could get a cabin steward to knock on the door with towels or something. He'd unlock the door and I'd follow him in before she can hide her intention, if she has any. If I caught her doing anything I'll just say I was worried and we want to keep her son under observation in the hospital because it might be contagious.'

It was a daring plan. But perhaps the situation called for it. 'What if she's in the shower or half-dressed?' There'd be hell to pay then. She tried to imagine the scene.

'Just before her appointment would be her most likely time for trying to exacerbate Tommy's rash.'

Tara shuddered. 'Do you want me to come?'

'Would you?' He thought about it. 'Maybe that could be better. If we don't catch her out this time, I don't want her to know we suspect her. You could say I asked you to look in because the clinic got busy suddenly. To save her waiting. Would you be comfortable doing that?'

'I guess.' Tara thought of the little boy who could be at such cruel risk. 'No. Not guess.' She lifted her chin. 'Of course I can. And it looks better if a woman forces her way into her cabin rather than a man.'

Nick rested his hand on her shoulder. 'Thanks,

Tara. I know you must be thinking this is pretty much out of left field but I let that other child down and I'm not letting this one suffer if it's happening.'

'I understand.' She did. Feeling like you'd let someone down was the worst feeling in the world. She looked at him. 'I would never have suspected this, you know, Nick. I would have let Tommy down too. And Wilhelm saw her yesterday.'

'It's a picture once seen never forgotten, I assure you,' Nick said grimly, and glanced at his watch.

Ten minutes later Tara knocked on the door of Gwen's cabin and the steward inserted the key in the lock. Tara drew a deep breath and pushed open the door.

Tommy was whimpering as his mother held his arm. Tara glanced and blinked at the label of the spray can that sat on the bench and bile rose in her throat.

She forced a smile and glanced away from the bench. How not to strangle the woman? 'Hi, Gwen. Remember me? Dr Fender sent me.' She made strong eye contact and Gwen stared back. 'Dr Fender is tied up with another patient but he asked me to drop in rather urgently.'

She strode forward and gently took the little boy's arm, which glowed angrily. 'He's had another thought about Tommy's reaction and it does seem red and worse. I think Tommy should come with me in case he's heading for an anaphylactic reaction. It could jeopardise his airway, you know.'

Tommy's mother bustled forward from where she'd fallen back at Tara's assertive stance.

'No. I'll bring him.'

Tara grimaced—as close as she could get to a smile—at Gwen. 'Perhaps you could find his pyjamas and medications and I'll meet you down at the hospital. I'm quite concerned, and I'm sure you are too.' The mother gaped as Tara picked up Tommy.

'But…'

Tara didn't wait to hear. She cradled the boy in her arms and carried him from the cabin. The steward followed her before she shooed him ahead urgently to hold the lift for them.

Nick was waiting and Tara rushed straight for the tap at the side of the room with Tommy in her arms. The little boy sniffed forlornly as she ran the cold water over his arm. 'Oven cleaner.'

Nick turned away and bunched his fist and then slowly straightened out his fingers until they were rigid with control. Not again. His stillness showed his feelings better than if he'd hit the wall, and he glanced at Tara to see if she'd noticed.

He couldn't help the past but he was damned

if he'd ever see anything happen like that again. He reached into the fridge and removed the white creamy burn salve that would soothe almost instantly.

Tara watched him gently comfort the little boy and Tara's heart squeezed when she realised the child expected it to hurt. 'Where does this sort of illness come from? I can't believe someone would do this to their baby.'

'Historically? It's a mental illness.' Nick's voice was low and gentle so as not to alarm Tommy. 'Psychotic behaviour. Maybe it happened to them as a kid. Or maybe they had no attention as a kid and it's turned into an irrational need. At this minute I don't care. All I know at the moment she will be diabolical with her lies and knowledge of conditions that backs up her imagined scenarios. When they do it to themselves it's bad—but to a baby like Tommy...' He shook his head.

'She'll be here in a minute.'

They both glanced at the door. 'We have to keep Tommy here tonight. The ship docks tomorrow in Mykonos and we'll have him transferred to the hospital. I'll ring them tonight and set it up.'

When Tommy's mother walked in her eyes were intense and fixed on Tommy with concern. Tara couldn't equate the woman she'd seen doing damage to her child to this caring mother. And just as hard to believe was Nick.

He spoke gently. Calmly, as if to Tommy. 'Sit down, Gwen. We need to talk about Tommy's rash.'

'What's wrong with him?' Gwen rushed over and cuddled the little boy who, to Tara's horror, snuggled up to his mother. 'Will he be all right? He's my whole life.'

'I believe you.' With those words Gwen seemed to settle and Tara tried not to let her mouth gape.

How could he say he believed her? Tara wanted to strangle her and discreetly she drew a deeper breath than normal to calm her own agitation.

Not discreet enough for Nick apparently. 'Do you think you could get Gwen a glass of water, Tara? Please. And send Gina in if you would.'

Tara nodded with relief while he glanced at the mum. 'I can see you're very anxious and we can't have you getting sick. Tommy needs you.'

It seemed this was the sort of appreciation Gwen needed because she relaxed into the chair Nick guided her to. 'Thank you, Doctor. You're very kind.'

'The thing is, Gwen,' Tara could hear him as she left the room, 'we'd like Tommy to stay with us tonight. Keep an eye on him, and I know that will be hard on you.'

The door shut behind her and their voices became a distant rumble.

'You okay?'

Gina, the nurse second in charge after Marie, was tidying the waiting room. The clinic was over and wouldn't open again for another two hours. They still had one child in the sick bay who was being nursed one on one by the other clinic nurse.

'We have another stay-over tonight.'

'The little boy with the rash?'

'Long story. Nick can tell you later.' She crossed to the water cooler and poured a paper cup full of water. 'Can you take this in for the boy's mother, please, Gina? Nick asked me to send you in. I'm going to look up something on the computer.'

'Sure. No worries.' Gina took the cup, crossed to the consulting room, knocked and went in. Tara stared as the door shut and shook her head. Tommy's mother was a darned good liar. In fact, Nick was a darned good liar too.

She tried not to dwell on the second thought

as she sat down at the computer but maybe she needed to remember his skills at fabrication when she looked at him next. Or maybe she should try not to look at him.

A bit like he hadn't looked at her that morning. And she had a horrible feeling it wasn't just Gwen.

But that was pretty hard considering what they'd shared last night. She only had to go within three feet of him and the hairs on her arms started waving hello to him.

She heard the key turn in the door Gina had locked at the end of clinic and Wilhelm poked his head in.

Tara gave a forlorn smile. 'Hello, there, chief. Are you supposed to be out of bed?'

He shrugged and smiled back. 'I'm the doctor. I said I could.' He narrowed his eyes. 'You okay?'

Tara nodded but couldn't dredge up any other

facial expression. 'Better than you, Mr Pale and Interesting.'

Wilhelm came in with purpose. 'I feel pale. But remarkably okay, actually. Must have been a twelve-hour bug. I just ate a horse and feel much better.'

'Poor horse.' Tara said it with a straight face and he frowned, worried. 'You're not a vegetarian, are you?'

Nick would have got it. Mentally she shrugged and couldn't help the thought about the last two years' staple diet of vegetable soup. 'Only when I have to. Loving the red meat here.'

It was Wilhelm's turn to study her. 'Suits you. More colour in the cheeks and not so bony.'

'Already.' Maybe her boobs would come back. Unwillingly she smiled. 'Better slow down, then.'

Wilhelm looked worried again that he'd offended her, and Tara held back a sigh. 'Nick's in there with a mum and her son. He's keeping the boy overnight.'

'Nick?'

'He replaced you for the last twenty-four hours.'

Wilhelm grinned. 'Nick's a champion. He's used to stepping in.'

She wasn't real sure if she needed to hear more glowing testimonials about Nick, not while she was wondering about how good an actor he was, but that didn't stop the curious part of her. 'So you two know each other well?'

'Last ten years. Catch up every couple of months at least. Depending where he's working and where I am.'

'So he's versatile?'

Wilhelm looked away and grinned. 'Oh, yeah.'

Enough. She didn't want to know. 'If you're determined to stay on I might take a walk, get some air.' She pointed to the computer screen. Her voice lowered. 'Better warn you this is what

Nick thinks is the problem…' she inclined her head towards the shut door '…in there.'

Wilhelm peered over her shoulder at the screen and she heard his indrawn breath as he scanned the page on a parent causing illness in a child to gain attention. 'Unpleasant. And Nick's sure?'

Tara sighed. The whole episode had upset her. 'I think she sprayed oven cleaner on her son. Makes me feel a bit sick, actually. I'll come back for afternoon clinic. That okay?'

'Sure. And thanks for holding the fort, Tara. Bit of a stressful introduction for you these last few days and you're due some extra time off. Not a lot of people who would have coped as well.'

Nick would have. Apparently. 'Thanks, Wilhelm.' She stood up and he slid into her seat to finish reading the medical article. 'Catch you later.'

Wilhelm looked up briefly. 'Sure. Don't rush. I can always page you.'

# CHAPTER ELEVEN

TARA drifted around the ship, trying to come to grips with Gwen's illness. With the idea that if Nick hadn't cottoned on, Tommy would still be suffering.

The hardest thing to come to grips with was the fact that he'd hugged his mother despite everything she'd done to him, and poor little Tommy was going to suffer when his mother was taken away.

Still, maybe one day Gwen could be well, medicated, psychoanalysed until she could be a safe mother again. Who knew what was in her own past? But at this moment Tara had trouble caring. The picture of Tommy squirming in the cabin haunted her. She couldn't help wondering what had happened to the child Nick felt he'd let down.

Tara did the whole walking track around the outside deck thing while most of the passengers were having their morning tea then climbed the stairs to her favourite place.

The bow of the ship, where most of the outdoor activities were grouped, always seemed semi-deserted. It was a good place to think, despite the mini-golf, half-tennis court, basketball rings. She walked past the two empty green tables and of course thought of Nick and his offer to beat her at table tennis and wished she'd embraced the simple things before it had all got complicated with these new feelings she was having for Nick.

Served her right for sleeping with him. Not that they'd done a lot of sleeping.

At least that morning since she'd been at work she hadn't thought much of last night, thanks to

Gwen, and suddenly her problems weren't as huge any more.

She glanced into the window of the children's play centre and saw the laughing faces as the teacher read a picture book. Poor little Tommy should be in there, not in a sick bay for protection from his own mother.

She wondered how Nick and Wilhelm were doing with Gwen and decided she didn't want to think about it.

She went down to the crew's dining hall and Miko was there with the first mate. He gestured her over.

'Come, Tara. Grace our table.'

Classic diversion. Why couldn't she have found Miko attractive? He was much less complicated than Nick. 'Hi, guys. What's happening?'

After an early lunch Tara returned to the clinic but her mind was on Nick when she unlocked the door and the sight that greeted her took a moment to sink in.

At first thought Tara assumed Gina must have fainted but when Tara fell to her knees beside her and rolled her over she saw the blood from the blow that must have knocked her out. Gina lay stretched out on the floor and as Tara's hand reached to staunch the blood she heard Wilhelm's raised voice.

'Take him, he's in the obs ward. Just get out of here so I can see to my nurse.' That was followed by an 'oomph' of pain and a crash, and Tara winced because the sickening thud boded ill for the recipient.

She needed help. Fast. She needed Nick. She scrambled for her phone and texted, 'Security, clinic,' and sent it before whoever was here could realise she'd sounded the alarm. She tucked the phone away quickly and glanced frantically around for somewhere to hide because footsteps were coming and there was no time to get out.

Too late. A wild-eyed Gwen burst from Wilhelm's office into the waiting area, wielding a metal stand used to hang intravenous fluids. She saw Tara, stopped and frowned as if confused, but it didn't last long enough as the element of surprise wore off.

Tara shifted backwards as Gwen launched herself at her just as Nick burst through the door and dived in to tackle Gwen to the floor.

In seconds Nick had Gwen pinned face down and, disarmed, and shortly after that four burly security guards arrived, followed closely by the officer of the watch.

The next few minutes were a blur as Gwen was heavily sedated, and Tara could feel her fingers trembling as she tried to staunch the bleeding on Gina's head.

After one fierce embrace to assure himself she

was unharmed, and a quick glance over Gina, Nick hurried through to Wilhelm.

An hour later Tara and Nick stood side by side as they watched through the window into Gwen's locked room. Deeply asleep, she'd been placed on monitoring while one of the security guards sat in the room with her. In repose her face seemed calm but Tara didn't think she'd ever forget the maniacal eyes of her attacker.

'You okay?' Nick was hovering.

Tara could tell he was upset she'd been in danger and she didn't know what to do with the feeling that she actually liked it that he cared enough to be upset. But he looked more than upset. He looked distraught.

She tried to reassure him. 'I'm okay. Thanks to you.' He really had dived right in. Anything else and she would have been flat on her back with a steel pole between the eyes. 'I couldn't believe how fast and powerful she was.'

Nick shook his head. Paced. 'No. I should have seen she was dangerously unstable. I thought we'd found a solution that would carry us through safely until we docked. I made an almost lethal mistake. Again!'

Tara put out her hand to catch his arm but he paced right past. 'You didn't make it on your own. Wilhelm agreed with you.'

'Wilhelm and Gina paid for it.' He jerked his hands through his hair and this time she reached out and touched his shoulder. His muscles were like steel bands, tension oozed out of him, and she slid her hand down and squeezed his upper arm until he looked at her.

'Looks like a fair amount of self-flagellation is going on here. Stop it. I'd say you've blamed yourself enough.'

Her hand dropped as she looked him up and

down. 'You'd probably have preferred to be where Wilhelm is now, nursing a sore head. Wouldn't you?'

'Too right.' He paced away from her again and then back, and she couldn't help the tiny whisper in her head that said she was sorry, but glad that it wasn't Nick on neurological observations in Room Two.

'Men!' She shook her head. 'I'm upset about Gina but relieved I'm not sporting a black eye or worse.'

'So am I.' He actually shuddered. 'Poor Gina.'

'Looks like we're back on duty together.' And here was a danger of a different sort. Not that she really minded as long as she kept reminding herself this was only short term.

Since that morning she couldn't deny that her body went into receptor mode every time she went near him. Now they'd be seconded in here together, again, with so many patients to stay and supervise, and she didn't know how that was going to go, not being able to touch him.

Today had left her feeling especially vulnerable. And not a little shaky. The idea of being cradled in Nick's arms, to find a haven of peace in a crazy world, and mutual comfort from a rather horrific day that had gone from one ghastly moment to the next, meant if he knocked on her door tonight she'd probably haul him in by the collar. And the idea was growing more attractive by the minute.

She wasn't quite sure if she was going to be able to hide that from him or whether she'd bother trying.

Nick was a mess.

The picture of Gwen almost smashing Tara with that pole played over and over in his head. He wanted to pull Tara into his arms and run away with her. Bare his teeth and keep her safe from crazy people. Protect her with his life. There was that life thing again.

Well, he couldn't. That wasn't who he was. So he shuddered all the way down to his toes at the thought of her being unsafe. And that was madness of a different sort.

He couldn't remember ever being so scared, well, yes, he could, but he'd been just out of med school then.

His mother. Dying in the hospital after the accident and all his brand-new skills hadn't been able to save her.

Then later, going through his parents' things, finding out his beautiful mother had had a secret. Written in her own handwriting, in his father's wallet, so he couldn't explain it away. That both their parents had lived a lie.

Of course he hadn't told the girls. Though he often wondered if Kiki knew somehow. God, he'd been wild, and bitter, and lost. And unable to tell anyone. He'd lost more than his parents that day.

Today had at least pointed out, with ironic fingers, how he was setting himself up to create the same mistakes his parents had made. The figment of an imaginary utopia. With Tara.

No way. How had he forgotten the basic rules? Don't get involved. Don't get attached. Good-time guy.

He had to get out of here before he cracked. 'Why don't you let me know if you get snowed under with work?'

He saw the confusion on her face and hardened his heart. It was for her good too. 'I'll do the call for night shift tonight.' He backed away towards the door. 'Keep Security here. I'll send another man down just in case. Page me if you need me. I need to check my other job.'

Nick barely saw the carpet on the stairs as he jogged up towards anywhere away from Tara.

Level after level. Upwards. Five floors, six, seven, eight, his breath starting to come a little more unevenly. Nine, ten, eleven, starting to pant now and he slowed to a walk. The plastered barman smile on his face was a caricature that would fool no one so he took himself to the stern and leant against the rail and breathed deeply.

He stared out over the green waves and felt the sickness of impending loss that he'd promised himself he'd never feel again.

He was in a dilemma. Last night with Tara had been incredible. She'd amazed him, reached him in ways nobody had ever reach him, had made him question his goals and expectations and want to be the man for her. But he didn't have the faith. Not in himself, not in life, not in relationships.

It wasn't fair to keep coming back for more, to be there when she turned around, to pretend he was laying foundations when he was really hoarding memories to carry away for when he was gone.

He knew it but couldn't stop himself.

He hadn't meant to go back to her cabin last night. Get in deeper. Fall more in love with the moments shared with her. But the clock was ticking until the cruise ended. Then Tara would be gone. He would be gone. They were both going to be miserable and it was all his fault.

What was going on here and how had he let himself get this entangled by a pair of long legs and a woman with an acquired phobia about death and disaster?

Then his initial agenda filtered in through his cold funk and he began to breathe again. He was just trying to help her. He could even feel his face relax with the thought. Okay. That wasn't so bad. He wasn't trying to fulfil her life, or his, he'd been trying to help. But now he needed to get out otherwise he'd be the one who needed help.

He just needed to ease away. Create distance again. Maybe a little diversion could put last night back into perspective.

Now he was kidding himself again. Last night with Tara had had the power to redefine his life if he let it, and that was what had rocked his mind this morning as he'd paced the deck. That and what he'd been going to say to her when she came down to work.

In the end Gwen had put paid to any discussions he might have had with her, and the reality of her being almost critically assaulted had destroyed his concept that it would be easy to walk away.

He didn't know what to do.

Back in the hospital, Tara listened to Nick's footsteps jog away. Nick had left? With a blankness in his eyes that said he wasn't coming back unless the walls fell in.

Tara frowned at the empty doorway and suddenly she felt alone, despite the half-dozen patients, the security guards and the need to start the quagmire of paperwork this incident had caused.

It was all very well for her to consider keeping her distance and then the rules had changed. It wasn't nice when Nick did it.

She wondered what this hollow pain in her chest was. Like someone had just scooped out her belly and let the wind in to whistle around.

Her hand crept to cover the cavity in her abdomen and she realised that Nick had the power to hurt her. Hurt her a lot. Perhaps more than her worst nightmare.

What had happened to that theory of spending time with Nick as a fast track to healing? Was this because of last night and the night before or in spite of it? But when it all came down to blame, she'd allowed it.

Tara winced and concentrated on the computer. Fool. That had been close. Imagine if she'd spent the next few days in his bed. She'd have been head over heels in love with him before they got to Venice. Well, she'd better snap out of it. No wonder he'd walked away.

Must have seen the threatening love light in her eyes. And discovered she didn't have much to offer. Just a hollow, damaged shell that had promised all she'd wanted was the quick fix of Nick holding her. Anyone with half a brain would be able to tell an empty shell wouldn't be enough for any man, let alone a man like Nick.

She sat at the desk and began to type up the incident. Concentrate. Document. Work.

Work had helped last time, until the cure had been worse than the disease. But she was supposed to be wiser now. Her mind went back to Gwen and the moment Nick had reassured the woman. The moment Tara had realised he could lie if he needed to.

She stopped and stared at the wall. But.

A part of her was whimpering, What if Nick had lied again? Like just now, when he'd made it obvious he just wanted to get away from her. It didn't make a lot of sense when she thought about it.

Because earlier, when he'd saved her, the expression on his face, the fierce hug he'd given her when he'd seen she was okay, that had said he cared. Really cared. What if he was just as scared as she was of being hurt?

Imagine.

Then the world intruded on her thoughts. Vaguely she realised the ship was rolling a little, like it had the first two nights she'd been on board. Not much, but enough to roll the pen off the desk and ensure she did a round to secure any loose objects.

Wilhelm was awake, and cross with himself for being caught unawares, and Gina asked for a cup of tea. No time to stew over her doomed relationship with Nick.

Then Miko arrived with an injury to his arm. 'You coming out tonight, sweet Tara? To dance?' Mico's chocolate eyes crinkled with mischief. Tara decided that cruise personnel certainly knew how to flirt.

'Not tonight, Miko.'

'Ah, but Mykonos is the party capital and we dock at midnight. The dancing is good. Very romantic.'

Tara laughed. 'You know I can't dance with you, Miko. You tread on my feet.'

'One mistake.' He threw up his hands. 'I could learn to dance with a dominant woman. The idea grows more enticing.'

Tara laughed. 'Yeah, right. But I'll be tucked up in my little bunk at midnight, after the last couple of crazy days.' She had a quick flashback to what she'd been doing last night and hurriedly picked up his chart and studied it. 'The only reason I'll be up is if there's a medical emergency.'

'Ah. So you are on call, then.'

Even though Nick had said he would do it she would be available, so she smiled and agreed as she taped the end of the bandage to Miko's damaged arm. 'We're down on numbers at the moment.'

'It is a shame you cannot come. The discotheques are very popular here and most of the crew will disembark and return around five in the morning.' His eyes appreciated her. 'It is not as if you need beauty sleep for you are already beautiful.'

Yeah, right. 'Maybe you shouldn't be going. You should rest that arm. It may not be broken but I'm pretty sure you've damaged ligaments.

What on earth possessed you to try and catch an urn that size?'

He shrugged philosophically. 'It is the centrepiece for my restaurant. I did not want it to break.'

'Next time let it go.'

When the night nurse came on to relieve her she knew she had to find out where she stood with Nick.

She just hoped he wasn't asleep so when she was standing in the corridor, waiting for him to answer his doorbell, she doubted her logic. This was dumb with a capital *D*.

But just as she turned she heard the door open and he was standing there, a towel slung around his hips, his hair tousled.

She thought at first it was okay but then his face changed and he didn't look pleased to see her. 'Déjà vu. Is this my turn for you to check on me?' he said.

No invitation, then. 'I wanted to know if you were okay.' The echo from yesterday was there and they both heard it. That was good, wasn't it?

Nick didn't say anything and she couldn't read his expression. Tara couldn't stand it any more. 'Can I come in?'

There was still no indication what he was thinking and she wished she could see just a glimpse of the Nick she'd met those first few days.

He shrugged and she winced. Even if he was pretending, it still hurt. 'Are you sure that's what you want?'

Tara felt a shaft of pain slice right through her followed immediately by a wave of heat in her face. He was knocking her back.

She spun on her heel and walked away and she could feel Nick's eyes on her. A rebuttal just like

Vander had given her many times, and never had she felt so mortified. Because Nick had made her believe.

A few seconds later she heard the cabin door shut.

Tara walked the length of the ship to the bow and felt the spray slap her in the face. Like reality. She'd been incredibly stupid. And blind. And she couldn't believe how gullible. But he'd never promised fidelity. Had said he flitted from month to month, changing girlfriends like socks. Well, he was sick of this pair obviously.

The bizarre part of it all was that if she could take back what had happened on the last two nights she doubted she would. How could she when Nick had made her feel like a real woman for the first time in her life? Maybe she just needed to leave some money at his door and then she could carry that into the future.

The guy obviously had a gift but she just wasn't cut out to be fast and loose—like him.

She guessed she'd known there were men like that in the world, she just hadn't actually met them. It was pretty hard to take.

She walked slowly back to her cabin where the memories were no easier to deal with but she assured herself the experience wouldn't kill her. Just toughen her up. Maybe that needed to happen.

Nick sighed and watched her hurry away. He shut the door and tried not to think about the distress on Tara's face.

Wilhelm's words floated back at him. 'I'd hate to see her hurt.' Well, he'd done that.

But since last night he'd been able to think of little else except how he was going to stay away from her.

# CHAPTER TWELVE

SPLIT, Croatia, and a beautiful blue-sky day. Tara decided to get off and get away from the damn ship. Create some distance between Nick and herself, if only for the day.

Wilhelm was again back on duty, looking a little the worse for wear, but just as determined for Tara to get away for the day.

A sedated Gwen had been picked up by an escort nurse and the coastguard for transfer back to Rome, and Tommy had been rescued by his aunt on Mykonos for temporary care.

Tara had been reluctant to hand him over without being sure his aunt was normal, but a bevy of giggling children in the car had helped, as did the children's services aide, who assured her she would be checking on his wellbeing.

Nick she didn't see, which was a good thing because, thinking about the next time he approached her, she wasn't sure how she'd handle that. Maybe sightseeing would help the emptiness she'd felt inside since she'd discovered the truth about Nick. After today there was only Venice and she'd seen little of the cities they'd visited.

She was still nervous about getting back on board if something went wrong, but the fact that if she climbed any structure above sea level she'd be able to see the ship helped.

She hailed a taxi.


Nick followed Tara off the ship and watched her stride along the long dockside car park to the taxi rank.

Nick's night had been plagued by regrets. How

badly he'd handled it. How much the hurt on Tara's face had replayed in his head. He'd been a fool and a coward not to tell her the truth.

He must have been insane to use Tara's visit as a golden opportunity to get out from a situation that freaked him.

Stupid, thoughtless oaf that he was, she'd never talk to him again and he couldn't blame her. But he needed to apologise and at least assure her she'd done nothing wrong. God, he'd crushed her just like her husband had done.

When he saw her climb into the taxi he picked up the pace and with two desperate strides opened the opposite rear door before they could drive off.

Tara considered opening her own door and climbing out again but the vehicle pulled away from the kerb.

'Please leave me alone, Nick.' She saw the taxi driver glance in the mirror and raise his eyebrows, and she wondered if he was offering to throw the extra passenger out. She doubted Nick would go peaceably but the gallantry made her feel a whole lot better and she declined the unspoken offer with a shake of her head.

Nick was oblivious to Tara's new protector. 'I will. Just as soon as I've apologised.'

She angled her shoulder towards him and gazed pointedly out the opposite window. 'For what? Being yourself?'

'You don't know me.'

She looked at him. 'Biblically?' She raised her own brows and he had the grace to glance away before he sighed and leaned her way.

'Look, Tara.' He lowered his voice. 'I'm sorry.'

She breathed in slowly and let it out. Felt a little of the tension she'd carried since yesterday ease away because breathing always helped.

But that didn't mean she was diving back in for a Nick-fest. 'Great. Can you get out now?

Or should I feel less brushed off as an annoying groupie of yours? Funny how I didn't like the feeling.'

She thought about it some more. 'So why was it easy for you to let me think what we shared was nothing?' That had stung and she glared at him. He was a low-life. 'Are we not even friends?'

Nick glanced up at the avidly curious taxi driver. 'Can we get out and talk about this?'

Should she? Tara checked with the taxi driver, who shrugged.

'Maybe?'

The man driving screwed up his face in the mirror.

Not decisive enough for him. 'Okay.' Tara gave in. Mostly because it had hurt so much when she'd thought Nick had been unmoved by something she'd almost call life-changing. 'We can walk into the city and then I'm going to have the rest of the day to myself. Here, thanks,' she said to the driver.

'Fine.' He owed her that. He glanced at the al-fresco restaurant on the edge of the park. 'It's our last stop before Venice, give me a chance, let me buy one drink as an apology, while I explain.'

She closed her eyes. It still hurt. Maybe she needed to hear. 'One drink. I don't want to force myself on you again.'

'You didn't force yourself on me, Tara.' That would be my undoing, Nick thought, and tried a smile. He could do light-hearted and platonic. He owed her that. 'Let's just enjoy the day. Like friends. The cruise will be over soon. Should we climb the bell tower?' And he would pay the price of another collection of memories to hold onto when she'd gone.

Tara loved bell towers. Was looking forward to the hundreds in Venice. There was even a voice inside her head that whispered she might even find the truth about Nick and herself up there.

Irrational, ridiculous, but so compelling it pushed her up the sharp steps, through the tiny tunnel built for smaller people hundreds of years ago and around and around through thick stone walls, feet gingerly climbing worn stone steps and sections of steep iron ladders that echoed and swayed, always enticing her up to the view she knew would be spectacular.

'Whoa. That was pretty hairy, coming up.' Nick was grinning, his hair blown across his forehead in an unruly heap, so handsome and devilish and so like her pirate that she ached just looking at him.

'So where do we go from here, Nick?'

'Back down again.' He didn't meet her eyes.

'Don't get me wrong. We both wanted a com-mitment-free two weeks of fun.' She waited until

262 A DOCTOR, A FLING & A WEDDING RING

he looked at her. 'So in two days we go our separate ways.'

'I hope we'll be in touch.'

She couldn't believe how much those words hurt. 'But without touching?' Why was she so surprised at being sad?

Tara looked woozily down from the church tower at the sprawling ancient city of Split below her, could feel Nick at her shoulder, and like the vertigo that had grown unexpectedly the higher she'd climbed the fear that what was between them was as flimsy as the guard rail that seemed so incapable of stopping her fall down the stairwell.

It had always been just a holiday affair. But what was really making her sad was how she was starting to believe that Nick would never find true happiness. And she wanted that for him, even if it wasn't with her.

'So can you tell me what happened? What made you like this?'

'Like what?' Stone walled Nick. Just like the tower.

'Come on, Nick. I know what happened to me. Indifferent parents. Difficult-to-please husband. Burnout at work. What spoiled you for happy-ever-after, Nick?'

She saw his shock. His assimilation of things she'd barely mentioned before but she hadn't said them to sidetrack him. Didn't want him side-tracked.

'There's something inside you that allows you to reach a certain point and then the safety catch kicks in.' She tilted her head and ignored the ver-tigo. 'What is that?'

She thought for a moment he was going to brush her off. They were alone, but she could hear the clatter of more people coming up the stairs. A very brief window of privacy. She almost didn't expect it when it came.

'A letter.' He shifted until he was beside her. His shoulder next to hers as he put his hands down to lean on the parapet. They looked into the city from above and it was like a thousand dolls' houses gazed on by giants. He didn't look at her.

'There was an accident. We were going through my parents' things after they died and I found a letter. From my mother to her lover. In my father's wallet so he knew. She'd been cheating for years, and I couldn't tell my sisters. They'd been heartbroken enough, so I burnt it.'

His voice was so quiet, unhurried, as if talking about someone else's tragic revelation.

'I burnt the proof that my parents' lives were a farce. That their marriage was a charade. I guess I lost my ideal of marriage that day, as well as my parents. I never told anyone. Then there was my friend's wife. Living a lie while she tortured her child. Two bizarre illusions of happy marriages I couldn't talk about.

'I just let it sit there and fester all these years. Became the good-time guy you see before you.' He tapped his chest. 'Definitely no plan for permanency.'

It wasn't what she'd expected but it made a lot of sense.

But it underlined the real reason they would never make it together. Trust. He didn't have any.

She looked away from his profile across the rooftops. An empty square with a gaping wound, the dome of ruined church vestry without a roof. Just grey walls going down into the dark hole with the hint of internal archways.

That's how her heart felt. Exposed and open, although the sun had turned to rain and now she knew what the future would be like without the comfort of a soul mate.

She sighed. 'My husband never trusted me. He'd had a failed marriage before me and I guess it came from there. I was young, idealistic and thought I could change him. He died before I saw any change but I think if he'd lived to be a hundred he'd never have changed. Never trusted me enough to open up and show me the real man.'

She sighed and looked away. 'Looking back I don't even think he trusted my medicine in those few months we had. I guess that was why I stayed. To prove to myself I really could help. Did have skills to offer.'

She could never again live with a man who didn't have faith in her. This would never work with Nick. Ever.

The vertigo increased exponentially. She could feel the ground rush up at her, along with the roaring in her ears. She swayed.

'Tara? You okay?' Saw Nick's concern tighten on his face.

'No. I don't think so.' The devastation was physical and manifested like a beast on top of the tower. Vertigo rose in her throat like hot bile. 'I don't think I can get down.'

Nick's concern was almost palpable but it didn't help. 'I'll guide you.'

If she didn't feel so sick she would have laughed. Nick couldn't guide himself. 'You can't help me, Nick.' Now she knew. All because of the letter found by a fresh young doctor.

She honestly hoped he'd heal one day.

Maybe talking about it today would help—down the track—too far away for her, though. 'At some stage you'll have to let go, Nick. Because that's what you do.' And she was talking about two journeys here. One down the tower and one into life.

She would be okay. She was strong. She might spin a bit but she knew her strength now. 'I'm better on my own.'

'That's not true. And has nothing to do with now anyway. Come on, I'll help you down.'

She shook her head but that wasn't good. Everything rotated so she stopped moving it. Or she'd throw up. 'No. I think I'll have to do it myself.'

Nick looked around for help, found none, saw the options and knew he'd have to do it her way. 'Then I'll follow you.'

'No. Go in front. At least I'll be able to see you.' Watch you walk away from me, she thought.

So he led, slowly, and she watched his dark hair float below her then pop back from around the curved walls to make sure she was still coming, and then he would go away below her on the steep steps.

She kept her hand on her flimsy rail and her eyes on Nick's hair. Once she slipped on the worn stone edge of an ancient step, and once she skidded down two instead of one, each time her heart in her mouth, but always her eyes returned to Nick's hair.

Funny. She could almost feel it under her fingers.

Then right at the bottom the section that was so narrow and steep she couldn't see him was upon her and his voice floated back. 'You okay, Tara?'

She couldn't answer, leant against the wall and breathed deeply for a few seconds. This was the last bit before it was over. She tried to move her feet forward.

'Come on.' His voice was beside her now as he gently took her arm. 'Nearly there.'

But once they got to the bottom she was going to say goodbye. They both should. Because the way she was feeling about Nick the unobtainable wasn't funny.

When they got to the bottom Tara reached out, squeezed his hand, said, 'Thank you, Nick, but

I want to go back to the ship alone.' Then walked away.

When he tried to follow she held up her hand to stop him and such was the resolution on her face he didn't follow.

Nick stood at the bottom of the cathedral steps and watched her go. What had just happened up there?

Nick started to walk back towards the dock where the tenders ferried people back to the ship.

Well, for a start he'd just told the first person ever about his mother's infidelity—something he'd never thought he'd blurt out up a bell tower—and admitted to Tara, and himself, that he wasn't looking to find the happily-ever-after he didn't believe in.

It sounded pretty stupid when you said it out loud. But there was no guarantee of lifelong fidelity. He'd seen plenty of examples on the ships

where he'd worked, and the hospitals he'd loc-
umed at that hadn't made him change his mind.

Relationships did fall apart. People were un-
faithful. Lies were told. Wasn't it better to know
up front not to expect too much? Then you
wouldn't be faced with the dilemma of creating
a web of lies that destroyed people.

'But this was Tara?' He said the words out loud
and he kept walking but he wasn't seeing the narrow stone archways and alleys of Split, he was
seeing his parents before he'd known, and for the
first time in a long time he just let the memories
come without judging. There were some pretty
good memories. Some great times they'd had as
a family.

But all the time the lies must have been there.

# CHAPTER THIRTEEN

NICK woke the next morning and stared at the ceiling. He wanted Tara. He ached for the gnawing emptiness of his arms. For the feel of her hair against his chest. To be able to run his fingers down over the contours of her head and across her silken cheek.

Something he'd chosen never to feel again. He wanted to hear her stride across the room with that determined walk of hers, a rhythm of footsteps he would never lose the memory of. The subtle scent of violets, his new favourite flower, a token he would never pass without seeing and feeling Tara's presence.

He was in love. Irrevocably. And he'd blown it.

With his new insight he just hoped that in the

past no women had ever felt like this about him while he'd been oblivious.

He wondered if his parents had felt like this when they'd first met. They must have because he had four sisters and a bag full of memories in their big old house that made him smile if he let them. About time he did.

Instead of the usual anger against his parents he only felt sadness. Poor them. To have lost this feeling would be the most tragic loss in the world.

He loved Tara and to hell with it. He'd rather have felt this and lost it than never felt it at all.

He looked out his porthole and saw they were coming into the waterways of Venice.

That first island greeted him. He always loved this moment and usually he was on deck for it.

A spot of land on the ocean, green and lush but not joined to the world of men.

He was sick of being an island. Admittedly

a party island but at the end of the day there was just him and his illusion of fulfilment and friends.

Maybe his parents had messed up, maybe they had broken each other's hearts, but at least they'd tried. He was the coward. He wanted to be so much more. For Tara.

The dawn touched her cheek on the pillow with grey-pink fingers of light, drawing her up to look out the porthole. Venice was coming.

Tara wanted Nick. Wanted to see the mischief in his face when he teased her, the solemnity in his eyes when he loved her. To feel the tenderness in his hands, those elegant, masculine hands that could be so powerful in protecting her yet so gentle with reverence when he touched her skin. She loved him. She knew that now.

Tara pulled herself up reluctantly in the bed, still in denial that today was the last day. A

breakwall made of rock—like a long bony finger—pointed towards the shimmer of the city
in the distance.

The waves slapped against the side of the hull
as they cut through the pastel water towards their
destination and the ship ignored the tearing pain
in her heart that wanted to plead with the captain to turn back out to sea.

How could she have fallen so deeply in love
with a man who couldn't love? What if she'd
been able to let go of the memories that had kept
her from being the woman Nick needed? Would
that have changed the outcome? Would he have
met her halfway? She'd never know.

Tara dressed silently, her face tight with distress, yet as always the tears stuck stubbornly in
her throat in a big dry ball.

She walked the full length of the ship through
the empty corridors. The passengers would be
packing last-minute hand luggage, all the cases

had lined the corridors the night before and were stowed below decks, ready for rapid removal and claim.

Passenger doors began to open. People moved towards the rails as the islands began to appear. Finally she reached the café at the bow.

She felt the rock in her chest grow heavier until it lay like a huge lead fist crushing her heart.

'Coffee, Dr Tara?'

Miko had a cup and saucer in his hand, his Slavic accent quietly kind with sympathy, and they shared a bitter-sweet smile.

She looked down at her cup. Her last cradle of fine ship's crockery, her last freshly brewed Colombian from a friend, a gesture of respect—and farewell.

'Thank you.' Her throat hurt from those unshed tears and the burning-hot coffee helped disguise that pain as it went down.

She put the cup down and climbed to the highest point on the deck, gazed out, and the breath stilled in her throat. The ship sailed blithely onward towards Venice.

Another island. Another. Ancient buildings, church spires, the increase of boat traffic. Vaporettos, water taxis, car-carrying ferries and tiny blue transport vessels.

More buildings as the sun rose and the ship drew nearer to the port. She stood there alone, no one beside her to share the moment, and she wondered if the rest of her life would be filled with moments with no one beside her.

Nick came upon her silently, stood for a moment oblivious to the landscape of Venice he normally adored, and absorbed the distress and loneliness he'd caused in Tara. He felt the sting of remorse and regret and sighed at his own stupidity.

How could she forgive him? He wasn't sure he could forgive himself. He absorbed her profile, saw how despite the pain she held her head high, shoulders straight as if she knew she would survive. This woman who had known such turmoil and heartbreak yet was still so strong.

His mind flashed back to the roadside scene when she'd first shown him her core of steel, and he loved her even more.

He prayed she could see he'd changed. That she'd encouraged that change by believing in him. Encouraging him to let the past go and stride into the future—hopefully with her.

But he'd understand if she said no. And he would be strong too, and try not to look back with regret but forward to new goals he'd avoided for too long. Thanks to a woman he'd once loved.

Suddenly the vista became overwhelmingly beautiful, spires and domes and long rows of arched buildings, snatches of greenery, and always the wash of the waves on the stone steps of an island as their ship glided past. This was the way to see Venice for the first time.

Sixteen stories above, gliding along the water, the whole orchestra that was Venice was laid out before her in the pastels and golden rays of sunrise.

Tara leaned back and closed her eyes. She wished Nick was there.

'I'm sorry, Tara.'

The breath jammed in her throat and she tried to swallow. 'Nick?'

'I'm so sorry I didn't tell you I loved you.'

She chewed hard down on her lip. She couldn't take his lies right now. 'What do you know about love?'

'Good question.' His voice came from behind her until he leaned down and kissed her. For a moment she weakened and shut her eyes and pretended.

He went on. 'I love you. It scares the living daylights out of me but when I wake up in the morning it's your face I want to see beside me. Every day.'

She turned and his smile and the light in his eyes blinded her more than the sun that lifted above the water, and suddenly she was unsure if this was a delusion.

'I dreamt of you big with my child.' A soft, sexy smile. 'Actually, there was more than one child.' Was this Nick saying these things?

Her heart seemed to be beating too loudly in her chest. Her face felt hot and then cold and she stared up into his face. The face she loved so much and had given up on seeing again. She saw the certainty there. But she couldn't believe him. 'When did you decide you love me? What happened to "long term isn't viable"?'

There was sympathy in his face. For the pain he'd caused her. And regret. And a promise to make it up to her. Shining out at her like the new dawn she'd just witnessed. 'I've let it go. Because I've loved you every minute since I saw you. I was just too frightened to admit it. And long-term viable isn't a quarter as scary as short term and gone.'

She looked around. The city was closer. Time was running out. 'Why now?'

He pulled her into his chest. 'Because I can't lose you. Can't have you disappear into Venice without me.' His voice dropped and his mouth came closer. He whispered, 'I know I'll want to feed you strawberries. And watch your mouth.'

She wanted to cry. For the tragedy of it all. But she couldn't. She wasn't worthy of him. Couldn't give him what he needed. A whole woman. Not a frozen hull of a woman.

I'll always love you, she thought, but she didn't say it. She watched the city grow through stinging eyes as it rose before her.

She hadn't expected Venice to be this achingly beautiful. Heart-wrenching, devastating, with Nick holding her right at this moment. His arms were around her and nobody else's would ever feel the same.

'It's okay to cry,' he whispered in her ear with her backed into his chest, hard against his hips, and her body recognised all of him.

When an unexpected sob tore from her throat she shuddered, frightened by the power of it, and he held her tightly, safely, and that was when the tears began to fall.

Suddenly she was drowning in a flood of silent, choking tears cascading down her cheeks as the glacier that had been frozen for the last two years began to crack and splinter and melt into flooding trickles of pain that dripped into the canals of Venice.

She wiped them away but more just soaked

her fingers and ran off her chin. Of course she hadn't brought a tissue.

'Here.' The handkerchief was pushed into her hand and she hid her face in the white cotton of his handkerchief as the floodgates opened even more.

As if Venice had released the gate to the torture she'd stored in her heart but, in fact, it had been Nick.

The faces of the people she'd lost, her husband who'd died an unhappy man, the babies who had never breathed, the men who had walked away broken because she'd failed their wives.

And the loss of Nick. But this man had not walked away, even though she'd failed him.

She cried for herself, and for Nick, and for the world she couldn't change, and Nick held her safe, gave her strength, warmed the last ice from her heart, and finally the weight eased from her shoulders. When she looked up from the safety of Nick's arms Venice was before her.

Wise and wizened, smiling with benevolence in all her aged splendour and determination to stay afloat. Like Tara and Nick would together.

They glided past the Doge's Palace silvery in the morning light, the huge tower of St Mark's Church soaring above the cobbles as the bells pealed a welcome, and she could see right into the almost empty square as they glided past the covered gondolas waiting for their morning passengers.

And then the sun blinded her as it rose above the horizon and she turned her head to rest her cheek against his chest.

Nick's finger came under chin and he turned her all the way and then lifted her chin. Her beautiful body was wedged against him and her scent wrapped him in a mist of lust and insanity. He breathed her in.

'I though you weren't doing this?'

He opened his eyes and studied the face he loved as she looked up at him. 'Well, that's the thing. I can't resist you.'

She smiled. Slowly and sweetly as she sighed into him. 'Damn,' she said as she kissed him.

'Welcome to Venice, my love. This is where we start our new life together.'

# CHAPTER FOURTEEN

Mr AND Mrs Nick and Tara Fender stayed in Venice for six months and when they left they left in style. The honeymoon suite on the rear of the Sea Goddess. A huge suite filled with flowers and baby clothes from the baby shower Kiki had hosted for them that afternoon with all their old friends on board.

Tara was gazing with delight around the huge cabin. 'Next year, when we've had our babies, and they're big enough, can we come back and cruise again?'

Nick couldn't think of anything he would enjoy more. 'I could work and you could play.'

'And Kiki might even have decided to leave the bar and head down to the hospital to join you.'

'I think she's nearly ready. But let's talk about us.' He lifted her fingers and kissed her wrist. 'I need to tell you something.'

The steward had just delivered their daily chocolate-dipped strawberries for the VIP couple and Nick leaned over the back of Tara's deckchair and held the strawberry above her mouth.

She giggled, and he swore he would never tire of that sound as he brushed the glistening fruit against her lips and then couldn't resist a taste. 'Yum. Strawberries, and not surprisingly chocolate ones, and best of all you.'

When they parted she held up her hands. 'No more. I swear you want me as fat as a pig.'

'Sweet wife, you eat two a day and only if I encourage you. It's not the chocolate that's putting on your inches.' He stroked a gentle finger down the mound of her stomach. 'It's our twins.'

Tara's hand floated down to rest on his and

their hands entwined as they both looked into the future that was as golden as the afternoon sun as they sailed out of Venice.

\* \* \* \* \*